D1438646

THE DAY THE QUEEN FLEW TO SCOTLAND FOR THE GROUSE SHOOTING

. . . is a taut political thriller which takes up the basic rivalry of today between the North and South of England and develops the theme to its logical conclusion: civil war. Atticus wrote in *The Sunday Times* earlier this year: 'The story starts with a football riot which breaks up the Newcastle-Chelsea final at Wembley. It highlights growing ill feeling between North and South which a Northern Committee has been trying to resolve peacefully. But some strong-arm men take over and organise a commando raid on London's BBC TV studios. The South send out a punitive force north to capture the leaders, but the old-school general in charge decides to teach Nottingham a lesson on the way and burns it to the ground. The Civil War is on. In York where the Mystery Play organizers have hired West End actors there's an alarming scene when the man playing Christ really is crucified. Now the Welsh back the North and they march on London, sweeping all before them. There's only one thing left for the PM and in the final chapter the South call in the Americans who come in and take over the country.

'It's a pretty disturbing story, but Mr Wise says there's an earnest moral behind it.

"Unless there is a massive decentralisation of government the difference between North and South has reached a point of no return." '

Other Books by Arthur Wise

NOVELS:

Days in the Hay
The Little Fishes
How Now Brown Cow
The Death's Head

NON-FICTION:

Reading and Talking in English
Your Speech
Communication in Speech
Spoken English for CSE
Talking Together
Weapons in The Theatre

THE DAY THE QUEEN FLEW TO SCOTLAND
FOR THE GROUSE SHOOTING

© 1968 *Arthur Wise*
First published in September 1968
by Cavalier Publishing Ltd.,
34 Upper O'Connell Street,
Dublin 1,
Ireland

PRINTED IN THE REPUBLIC OF IRELAND
BY HELY THOM LIMITED, DUBLIN

TO NAN

FOR EVERYTHING

ACKNOWLEDGEMENTS

I am grateful to the following for their advice during the preparation of the manuscript:

Keith Liversidge for information on the Civil Service.
Bill Tate for information on the Oxford Colleges.
Lt. Colonel Northover, Leeds University OTC, and the Army Information Office, York, for advice on Army structure and weapons.
Bryan Mosley for advice on the internal structure of the Wood Lane TV Centre.
Robert Patterson, Eric Hope and the staff of the Castle Museum, York, for a great deal of information essential to the story.

I am grateful to Mrs. Betty Simmonds for her help in preparing the typescript, and to Miss Sonia Brownell and Secker and Warburg Ltd. for permission to reprint the extract from 'The Road to Wigan Pier' by George Orwell.

I am particularly grateful to my wife, Nan, for having read the manuscript so many times and making so many invaluable comments on it.

ARTHUR WISE, York, 1968

THE DAY THE QUEEN FLEW TO SCOTLAND FOR THE GROUSE SHOOTING

A Document by

ARTHUR WISE

CAVALIER  PUBLISHING

DUBLIN

. . . we have turned our backs on our Victoriad, excluding industrial history from our art and education, treating the North as a waste-land beyond reclaim. Because of it, Northerners remain a resentful enclave of our population, convinced that their part in our history has never properly been recognized, that Britain is as much two nations today as when Disraeli published *Sybil* in 1845.

RONALD BRYDEN: *The Victorian Miracle*

Nationalism is essentially a matter of values in personal life.

For many, the death of a nation and the awful waste of great moral and spiritual resources matter nothing as long as people are well fed, well dressed and well housed.

GWYNFOR EVANS

'The iron fist must come down. We haven't thrown up a Grivas yet, but the situation is ripe for one. Then the English Government will have to repress the people and Welshmen will have to take sides.'

quoted by COLIN MCGLASHAN in
The English Reconquest of Wales

But when you go to the industrial North you are conscious, quite apart from the unfamiliar scenery, of entering a strange country. This is partly because of certain real differences which do exist, but still more because of the North-South antithesis which has been rubbed into us for such a long time past. There exists in England a curious cult of Northernness, a sort of Northern snobbishness. A Yorkshireman in the South will always take care to let you know that he regards you as an inferior. If you ask him why, he will explain that it is only in the North that life is 'real' life, that the industrial work done in the North is the only 'real' work, that the North is inhabited by 'real' people, the South merely by rentiers and their parasites. The Northerner has 'grit', he is grim, 'dour', plucky, warm-hearted and democratic; the Southerner is snobbish, effeminate and lazy—that at any rate is the theory. Hence the Southerner goes north, at any rate for the first time, with the vague inferiority-complex of a civilized man venturing among savages, while the Yorkshireman, like the Scotchman, comes to London in the spirit of a barbarian out for loot.

At the back of the mind of every Yorkshireman and every Scotchman who comes to London is a sort of Dick Whittington picture of himself as the boy who starts off by selling newspapers and ends up as Lord Mayor. And that, really, is at the bottom of his bumptiousness.

When I first went to Yorkshire, some years ago, I imagined that I was going to a country of boors.

There is nevertheless a real difference between North and South, and there is at least a tinge of truth in that picture of Southern England as one enormous Brighton inhabited by lounge-lizards. For climatic reasons the parasitic dividend-drawing class tend to settle in the South.

GEORGE ORWELL: *The Road to Wigan Pier*

Having just returned from spending the holiday with a working-class family in a fairly large Northern town, I'm not surprised that the 'I'm Backing Britain' campaign started in the South. What a contrast there is between the North and the South!

The majority of Northern men do not appear to have any interest in the state of Britain. Their only concern seems to be in getting plenty of money to spend in 'the club' and on gambling.

'Wilson and his lot' were blamed for foot and mouth and for the wine and spirit shop selling out before the New Year!

As for men helping in the home—no wonder the women have lost interest.

Incidentally, I had heard a lot about the wonderful Northern cooks but I didn't meet any. The only vegetable cooked by the majority was the potato. And the only pies and cakes eaten were bought from the numerous pie and tripe shops which flourish alongside the betting shops.

'Live for today' seems to be the Northerners' motto.

'PROUD SOUTHERNER', Battersea, London s.w. 11.
Live Letters, *Daily Mirror*, January 12, 1968.

"In the North we are beginning to feel more and more neglected." LORD DERBY, May 13, 1968

PROLOGUE

THIS document is an attempt to piece together the disastrous events of the past year, from existing reports and from personal interviews. Where it has seemed to me the most effective way of giving the reader a clear understanding of the situation, I have simply set down the bald facts. In other places, where I have had supporting evidence from interviews, I have attempted to reconstruct actual conversations and events in such a way as to convey the total feeling of them.

It has been no part of my intention to offend anyone, nor to apportion blame. Nor have I attempted to interpret the facts, beyond the point where some interpretation of them has been essential for an understanding of the situation, and could be supported by evidence. Nonetheless, I must acknowledge that I am a Northerner, and that this is necessarily a Northern statement. I am well aware that a similar document by a Southern writer might well be very different.

In one or two places, I have had to suppress some of the facts, simply to make my own position and that of my friends in the North, still tenable during the present period of occupation. This suppression in no way affects the general accuracy of the report.

I am most grateful to Brigadier John Macey, at present still in hiding in the North, and to Mrs. Valerie Paine, now living in the south of France, for allowing me to talk to them about the events in which they were both so deeply involved.

ARTHUR WISE, York

1

To anyone returning to the North last year after a long absence, the atmosphere of the place had changed. Not changed, perhaps, rather crystallized. Hardened; become more coherent. A man, living all his life in Leeds or Bradford or Manchester, might not have noticed the difference. It had all been gradual enough. Gradual but none the less a difference. Suppose you said to such a man, 'What changes have you seen in your lifetime here?' What would he say? Well, there were the trams that clattered through the traffic down Briggate. They had gone. The horse-drawn waggons that trundled Josuah Tetley's beer over the cobbled back streets. They had gone, more or less. Most of the gas lighting had gone, though not quite all. There was the traffic and the one-way streets and the tall blocks of flats, replacing the acres of back-to-backs. But Artist Street and Mario Street were still there, and Blackman Lane. Washing was still strung above the cobbles of Lavinia Street. The Town Hall stood as black and forbidding as ever at the bottom of the Headrow.

These were differences, of course. But they were not what struck the returning exile most forcibly. To that man, getting off the train at City station and emerging bag in hand into City Square, it was the atmosphere. He could sense it at once. It was in the stance of the policeman directing traffic in his long white coat. He could sense it in the cry of the man selling the city edition of the Yorkshire Evening Post outside the post-office. It was there in the faces of people in the bus queue. If he could put it into words, what would he say? He might tell you there was a certain assurance about the place. Arrogance, he might call it. Here is a town, he might tell you, that seems at last to have grasped an identity, that has come to terms with what it is, that sees itself as a unique entity with a life different from that of any other place on earth. A town rising up out of the filth and rubble and exploitation of the nineteenth century and opening its eyes for the first time. Self-conscious and aware. Critical and dissatisfied. Bitter, perhaps. Certainly determined to find a place for itself in the sunlight, and in the eyes of God. He might go further; he might tell you, if you had no Northern blood in your veins, to tread warily through those streets, to keep your eye on the man next you in the bus queue and to sleep with your window closed, for there was revolution in the air.

Stephen Jackman wrote a brief letter to the *Times* that May morning. He had heard a cuckoo calling from the woods near his home. The call had that odd, cracked quality characteristic of the bird in July. It seemed a sufficiently rare phenomenon to deserve the notice of those readers of the *Times* who are interested in such things. The occurrence, and his letter, impressed the date in his mind. It was May 5th. When he left the house on his way to the meeting of the Theatre Building Committee in York, he took the letter with him. He intended posting it after the meeting.

Jackman was 48; tall, lean, the bone structure of his face prominent and large. A classicist—he preferred the word 'classic'—born in Bolton and educated at the Grammar School and Manchester University, now with a lectureship in the University of York. Rather slow, careful and deliberate in speech, but with a dogged and unshakeable determination on any matter of principle. He was a man in every way reliable. A man whose friendships, once made, would last unshaken to the end of his life. A man, deserted by his wife some two years earlier, and left now to bring up two young children alone.

Of the 14 members of the Committee, 10 were already there when Jackman arrived. It was 11.10 in the morning. Jackman thought it was uncomfortably hot in the little hall, converted from the nave of one of the city churches. He was wearing a suit of heavy tweed, whose trousers never held a crease because of the thickness of the material. He wished he had put on something lighter. He took out his pipe and began to fill it. 'I suppose we can smoke in here?' he said to Councillor Mrs. Adams. He had a profound respect for the tradition embodied in the church. Councillor Mrs. Adams was a heavy woman in her early sixties. She had been a supporter of the Labour movement and Trade Unionism from her teens. 'Strike a match in here,' she said, 'and you'll blow the roof off.'

Jackman didn't understand. 'Oh?' he said, the bowl of his pipe still stuffed inside the pouch.

'Haven't you heard?' said Mrs. Adams. 'The Minister's refused the application.'

Dr Blackett pushed through the swing doors at 11.15, and walked to the front of the hall. He dropped a folder on the table, stared for a moment at the stained glass window that had once been over the altar, then turned round and dropped into the chair. 'Let's get started,' he snapped, and took the papers from the folder. Members of the Committee looked at one another. They had seen Blackett in this mood more than once.

Blackett, despite the fact that he had been in practice in the town for more than twenty-five years now, was still something of an enigma. His behaviour was unpredictable. He could, on occasions be extremely rude. He could, and at times, did, cut down his hostess at a party with half a dozen grossly insulting words. And yet he continued to be invited to social functions. He was actively feared by many of his patients. He gave the impression of suspecting that everyone who sought medical advice was a malingerer. And yet he still had the fullest surgery in town. Fear and awe were probably the two commonest emotions felt by his patients. It was rumoured, with some justification, that his denigrating and vicious remarks had reduced his wife over the years to little better than a hysterical wreck. Certainly no one ever saw her now outside the grim, unpainted house where they lived. It was rumoured, too, that he was embittered by a lack of recognition. True, he could scarcely have been a more successful General Practitioner in a town with little over a hundred thousand inhabitants. But he had lived to see his contemporaries at Guy's pluck the plums of London consultancies. Meyer, as near to being a friend of

Blackett's as anyone could hope to come, was now a consultant physician to the Royal Family. He had done no better than Blackett in 'finals'. When Blackett heard the news, he wrote to Meyer suggesting that his renown must be the result of some underhand practice. Meyer was too upset to take any action. The view held in professional circles in the town, was that Blackett had slipped into political activity in the hope of achieving the recognition that medicine had denied him.

'For those of you who don't know,' said Blackett, without any preliminaries, 'our application's been turned down.'

'But good God why?' said Jackman.

'Why!' snapped Blackett. 'What a damn' silly question. For the usual reason of course. Because we live two-hundred miles from the seat of government—am I the only one who can see that?'

'Ridiculous,' said Jackman, very deliberately. 'Can we hear the letter?'

Blackett glared at him as if he could have struck him dead. Jackman was quite immovable; quite uncompromising. At last, Blackett took up the letter from the pile of papers in front of him. 'Very well,' he said. 'It's addressed to me. The date's the fourth. "Dear Sir, The Minister wishes me to thank you for your communication of April 15th, requesting a grant in connection with your theatre rebuilding programme. I am instructed by the Minister to inform you that because of the economic difficulties that the country is facing at the moment, no grant can be made to you in this connection, etcetera, etcetera." Well?'

'Is that all?' said Jackman.

'That's all.' He threw the letter on the table and took a long drink of water from the glass at his side.

'What about Manchester? They made a similar application.'

'Turned down. I rang Phillips this morning.'

'And High Wycombe—the Civic Arts proposal?'

'I'm waiting for a 'phone call now.'

'It must be turned down,' said Jackman. 'There can't be any exceptions.'

'Why not?' said Blackett. 'It's less than thirty miles from Wycombe to Hyde Park Corner. Grounds enough there for an exception to be made.'

Miss Lidgett-Evans stood up. She was a teacher of dance, dressed entirely in black. Under the artificial lighting of the dim hall, even her lip make-up seemed to be black. Her speech had that refined veneer to it, that is more common in the North than in the South. She said: 'I wonder if you are aware, Mr. Chairman, when you make these disparaging remarks, that the Minister was born in Rotherham and brought up there?'

'I wonder if *you* are aware,' growled Blackett, 'that he now lives in Hampstead and frequents the better-known clubs of St. James?'

'Well,' said the reverend John Boyd, running a finger round the top of his collar. 'What do we do now?'

'We fight,' said Blackett, simply.

Blackett admitted later that when he made the statement, he had no idea what it would actually mean.

Blackett received the 'phone call he was expecting, at home.

'It's for you, Colin,' said his wife, holding out the receiver for him to take. 'It's Mr. Peters I believe—from High Wycombe.'

'Give it to me,' said Blackett, 'and for God's sake stop dithering about.'

'I'm sorry, Colin—I thought . . .'

'This is a private call,' said Blackett, his hand over the mouth-piece. 'Do you mind?'

'I'm sorry,' said Mrs. Blackett. She paused for a moment. He looked at her, waiting. At last she left the room, closing the door so quietly behind her that he heard no sound from it at all.

'Thought you'd like to know, old man, that they've given us the grant after all,' said Peters.

'How much of it?'

'All—the whole blessed lot! We can start building right away. It's a major break-through, old man.'

'Of course. They've turned us down—old man,' said Blackett, putting the 'phone down.

At lunch, Mrs. Blackett said: 'Don't take it too hard, Colin. I know how important it is to you, but it isn't a major disaster is it? And the country is in a bit of a mess—financially, you know. They had to prune somewhere. I don't suppose they see a theatre building project as something of national importance.'

'I suppose so,' said Blackett.

'Hm?' said Mrs. Blackett, not quite understanding.

'Hadn't you better rest?' said Blackett. He was wondering how he could get to the Minister.

Blackett was quite clear in his own mind about the Theatre Building Committee. He rarely went to the theatre himself. He had little interest in any of the arts as such. Whether in fact the theatre had these proposed extensions or not, was in itself quite unimportant to him. He saw the committee as a tool, a mouth-piece, through which a neglected and depressed community could at last make itself heard. As far back as 1966, he had said to a meeting of doctors in Harrogate: 'Make no mistake about it, the central government rules for the south-east, not for us. Medical practice is laid down in Harley Street and the Central Middlesex, and we are expected to follow it without question. Second-rate citizenship begins north of Hitchin.'

He saw himself really as one of the rare vocal members of a deprived and underprivileged nation. The North. At that time he saw the frontiers rather vaguely. Sometimes the southern frontier ran just south of Doncaster, at other times it fell just north of Barnet. He confessed later to a certain Messianic sense of destiny, a feeling of carrying with a handful of others the responsibility of lifting a community into the sunlight. 'London,' he said, 'is where the blossom and the fruit are. But the roots are here. We want at least some of the pickings from our own tree.' Blackett was rare in being able to verbalize his feeling so clearly. But the feeling itself was shared by millions of others. The North was beginning to stir.

The Cup final that year took place on May 12th. How far the

scenes there contributed to the final disaster, it is impossible for anyone to say. Certainly it would have been difficult at that time to have picked two teams likely to have produced a more explosive situation. Newcastle United and Chelsea were focal points of totally opposed views of life. Harry Oldman, a newsagent in Shepherd's Bush, said in an interview on TV Colour after the match: 'They were a bunch of bears come down from the wilds.' To the average Northerner, Chelsea was synonymous with the plush life; rich, amoral. The very name was offensive to Northern puritanical ideals. A girl of 15, appearing in Dewsbury Juvenile Court said: 'I ran away to London because there's nobody to stop you doing what you want. You can go to parties in Chelsea and places and stay up all night if you want. Nobody cares what you do. You can have fun.' The Chairman of the Magistrates said: 'Life is not just having fun. It's a very serious business. If you want to get on you've got to work. What you've told us is not only immoral but wrong.' The Chairman might have been summarising much of the Northerner's attitude to the South.

Wembley Stadium held more than 100,000 people that day. It was, on the face of it, a perfect day for the peak event of the English football season. The temperature was in the high sixties, the sun was warm without being uncomfortably hot, there was the merest breath of a breeze and a few rolls of white cloud hung steadily to the south. There was nothing to anyone but the most perceptive observer, to suggest that there was anything different in the scene or the atmosphere from any cup-final that had taken place before. But this most perceptive observer would have noticed the tensions at those points where the supporters of the two teams came most closely into contact with one another. There was an antagonism at these points, an aggressiveness, that had nothing to do with allegiances to particular teams.

The preliminaries ran along the well-worn lines. The bands, the organized cheering, the mass singing. A large group of Newcastle supporters, high up behind one goalmouth, did try to break the massed hypnotic chanting of 'Abide with Me' by singing 'Billy Boy' and 'Blaydon Races' at the tops of their voices. But there was no chance for them against the wave of ninety-odd thousand opposing voices. An attendant standing behind them, John Blower of Edmonton, said: 'They had some cases of Newcastle beer that they must've brought with them. They kept opening bottles and passing them round. I thought they were drunk. I doubt if anyone but me noticed.'

Certainly Charlie Kane from Brighton, the leader of the singing, noticed nothing. 'They didn't even need me,' he said afterwards. 'They knew the words and the tunes and they started themselves off. As far as I was concerned, it went like clockwork. I did nothing but stand up on that platform in the middle of the pitch and wave my arms about to keep them in step.'

The teams came out, loosened up for a few minutes and then lined up to be introduced to the Prince of Wales. There was a good deal of cheering and a few isolated cat-calls. Play began at 3.15 p.m. It ran back and forth, first in the Chelsea half then in the Newcastle, for twenty minutes. During that time neither goalkeeper touched the ball once. It looked as if it was going to develop into one of the duller cup finals. Then, in the twenty-fourth minute, Burnham of Chelsea brought down the Newcastle inside-right Allerston, just inside the penalty area. The ball spun away and ran over the goal-line. The whistle blew and the referee, Stanley Armitage of Huddersfield, pointed at once to the corner post. Every responsible person in the stadium agreed that the decision was right. Wilson of the 'Mirror' said: 'From where I was sitting, it was the fairest tackle I've ever seen.' Tony Richardson, who had come down from Darlington to report the match for the 'Northern Echo' said: 'The referee was absolutely right to give a corner. There wasn't the slightest question of Allerston being fouled.' Even Allerston himself, questioned by an ITN reporter that evening said: 'I've no grievance. Burnham really went for me, but it was a fair tackle. I tripped over his foot, but that wasn't his fault.'

Stanley Armitage said: 'The second I pointed to the corner post I knew something was going to happen. You get hardened, you know. Normally you don't notice the crowd. It's something that's there, but you don't really notice it. But you couldn't ignore this. It seemed to rise up in the stands all round you. I remember looking round just before Lawson went to take the kick. It was like looking round at a thunder storm that was closing in on you. I remember feeling cold. It seemed to move in on to the pitch. Then it was on top of me. I remember seeing one or two faces quite clearly. Some of them were going for my head with bottles. Two of them I might have handled, three perhaps—I was a boxer, you know; pretty useful—but not that lot. Not in that mood.'

Andy Watts was commentating for BBC TV. The actual recording was lost when the Wood Lane TV Centre was burned down in the attack on London in June, but Watts says: 'I don't need a recording to remind me of that day. I was in the commentator's box keeping an eye on the monitor. It was a perfectly good tackle, I could see that. The producer cut in to the referee in close up. He pointed straight to the corner flag. Something made me look up. It must have been the atmosphere. It's an odd position in that box. You can see the crowd and you can hear it, but you're not part of it. You see it as something separate. But I could feel it too. The way you might feel the presence of some dangerous animal in the dark. I remember keeping up some sort of patter while I was looking around. I knew the cameras would be following somebody—Lawson probably—to the corner flag. I could hear some shouts from the crowd, the kind of things you get used to: "Foul!" "Penalty!" —the usual things. Then the Newcastle supporters behind the Chelsea goal began to chant: "Dirty bastards, dirty bastards." It went on and on, with an insistent rhythm that made you begin to nod your head in time with it. I'd never heard anything like it, and I've covered hundreds—literally hundreds— of sporting events. It was like a physical wave of sound. It pulsed through the air. I remember wondering: would a bird manage to get through it? Then I noticed it had changed. It had changed to "Southern bastards, Southern bastards". Others began to join in. Others, I suppose, down from the North. And the volume had increased, though a moment before I hadn't thought it possible.

'In the stand opposite, fighting had broken out at the point where Chelsea and Newcastle supporters met. From the place where I was sitting I couldn't make out any detail, but police were running along the touch line and climbing up through the crowd. I looked at the monitor. I knew that at least some of the cameras must be picking up the scene, but the picture showed nothing but Lawson standing at the corner flag, hands on hips, waiting for the referee to give the signal for the kick. All the time I kept up some kind of patter, but I didn't know what to say with the monitor showing nothing but a relaxed player hands on hips.

'Then the whole mass of spectators began to move from behind the Chelsea goal. It rolled down on to the ground, like lava from the lip of a volcano. It felt about as hot. Police ran up and began waving to the mass. People climbed over the crush barriers. I saw one barrier just cave under the weight. The police disappeared under the rolling wave of people. I didn't see how they could emerge alive, facing the wrong way and trying to impose some order and control on to what had become a united, determined animal. Of course, as we know now, many of them didn't.'

Reports are confused, since most people in the stadium were involved more or less in some part of the action. They have clear memories of a minor incident, but little idea of the whole movement. Harry Verney, a Ford worker from Dagenham and a Chelsea supporter for years, said: 'I was lucky. I was in the middle of a Chelsea mob and managed to get out of the ground without being touched. But I saw a bloke with one of those ice-cream trays round his neck. They just picked him up and slung him over the edge of the tunnel where the players come out.'

It is significant that Verney referred to the group of Chelsea supporters he was with, as a 'mob'. No one can deny that the violence began with the Newcastle supporters behind the Chelsea goal. Equally, it is undeniable that once violence had been triggered off it spread throughout the ground. Watts, sitting in the comparative safety of the commentator's box, saw 'the entire ground seething'. 'The grass,' he said, 'disappeared under the sheer numbers of human beings. From where I was perched, out of it thank God, it was like watching a stirring, writhing mass of maggots at work on the dead body of a rabbit. Occasionally I could make out an individual—usually a player in a black and white or blue strip—struggling to get clear of it down the tunnel or out of the ground. But mostly, actual individuals had disappeared.'

By 4.30 p.m., when police had arrived in sufficient numbers to begin imposing some order on the scene, most spectators were clear of the ground and the fight had gone out of those who were left. They sat on the terraces nursing broken heads and cut faces. Some fifty or sixty people lay prone on the pitch, on their faces or on their backs. Lawson, the Newcastle winger, had been impaled on the broken corner post. The royal party, the PM and most of the officials, had got clear soon after the trouble started, but Bert Tidmarsh the Chelsea manager was found at the foot of the stand with his back broken.

Detachments of police were put on all trains from King's Cross back to the North. Passengers, for the most part, were subdued, though the body of Constable Wright of the Hendon detachment, was found on the track between Peterborough and Grantham at 10 o'clock that night. He had been pushed through the window of a moving train.

In Darlington, Middlesbrough, Sunderland, Newcastle, police patrolled the platforms as the trains came in from the South. But there was no trouble. Nothing at all. For the moment the crowd seemed purged. 'You'd have thought they were coming from an Easter service,' said Sergeant Bland, brought in from Durham County to reinforce the Newcastle police.

Tony Richardson remembers sitting in his office in Darlington that night, trying to write a piece for the Monday edition. 'I was like a dream' he said. 'Darlington was as quiet as the grave. Saturday night, and not a single drunk singing in the street outside. Those scenes a few hours earlier. That violence, generated by a simple game of football. But I had the strange feeling that if I could see the thing whole, I'd notice a certain logic about it—a certain justice even. I remember saying to myself, quite out loud: "Odin is climbing into the saddle again —after all these years." I wrote: "Make no mistake. What we witnessed on Saturday was a little blood-letting, no more." It was prophetic.'

2

ALL formal meetings at Number 10 are, of course, minuted. Circulation of these minutes is highly restricted. There is no way in which we may know precisely what was said at the meeting on the morning of May 13th. It may be another fifty years before an historian is given access to the necessary documents. Downing Street was not then closed to the public and the Press, and film taken at the time shows who went into the house between 9.30 and 10 that morning—at least through the front door. In addition to the Inner Cabinet, the following people appear to have been present:

Major B. B. Hobbs, Director of Security to the Royal Household.

Alex Surtees, administrator responsible for security arrangements at Wembley Stadium.

Robert Paine, Second Secretary to the PM.

Arthur Pratt, Minister of Transport.

John Evans, Director of Security, British Railways.

Lt. General Sir Darwin Fitzroy Blakney, Commissioner of Police, Metropolitan Area.

Andrew Gerraint, Chief Constable of Middlesex.

Lt. Colonel James Patterson, Chief Constable of Hertfordshire.

Sir Vainey Matthews, Chief Constable of Buckinghamshire.

Brigadier Sir Latimer Maitland, representing the CIGS.

From the official statement made to the Press after the meeting, from subsequent events and from a source who for obvious reasons cannot be named, it is possible to reconstruct the meeting with some accuracy. The PM did not go into the room until 10.10. It was obvious to everyone, as he thrust open the

door, that he was taking the Wembley incident with extreme
seriousness. One reason, no doubt, was that, since he himself
was a Northerner he felt this as a personal affront. Another was
the fact that this was not an isolated incident, although it was
certainly the most dramatic. Brigadier Maitland, on the other
hand, saw the Wembley affair as entirely isolated. He was of
the opinion that the army should have been called in the
moment the crowd was seen to be out of hand. 'At that moment,'
he is supposed to have said, 'the whole business could have been
crushed in fifteen minutes by one competent Company.' He
talked of 'making an example of the ringleaders.' It is an
indication of the caution with which the PM approached the
situation that morning, and of the implications that he saw in
it, that Maitland left London three days after the meeting to
take up the command of the Overseas Army Training Centre
at Plymouth on the personal orders of the PM.

'The crucial point to decide,' said the PM, his pipe held
just clear of the corner of his mouth, 'is the extent to which
this is an entirely isolated incident, and the extent to which it
represents a much more widespread feeling of discontent. My
own opinion is that the latter is nearer the truth.' He turned
to Blanshard, Minister for Home Security. 'Minister?'

Blanshard was young for Cabinet rank. He was 39, a product
of Downing where he had read English under Norman Peel.
He was unmarried and looked almost ten years younger than
his real age. No one denied his intellectual brilliance; it was
principally for this that the PM had chosen him for his present
office. But there was a certain theatricality about his manner
that the PM had always found irritating. There was nothing
of that statesmanship and wide vision that characterized the
PM himself, about Blanshard. His habit of throwing back his
lank, fair hair with a supple twist of his head, the PM found
particularly irritating. His image on TV was described by
many people as 'affected'.

'I am reminded of the 20s and early 30s,' he said. 'From what
one has read, only a very few, isolated incidents of the General
Strike of '26 bear even the remotest comparison with yesterday's
incredible incident. Consequently I'm at something of a loss
as to what advice I can usefully offer.'

'There was a pattern then,' said the PM. 'The General Strike—since you mention it—the Jarrow March. You don't see these as unrelated?'

'Oh no. Certainly not. They arose from a sense of class deprivation. Intimately related, of course. Peaks of the same iceberg. I can see no such pattern in the present situation.'

'An isolated incident, you think?'

'Entirely,' said Blanshard, with a dismissive wave of the hand.

With the exception of Sir Darwin Blakney, Commissioner for the Metropolitan area, the police were not prepared to commit themselves on the wider implications. Sir Darwin, who had had considerable overseas experience, said: 'I think, Prime Minister, that there's a good deal of sense—er, you know what I mean: truth—in what you say. Now I've no *facts* to support me. No doubt there are some. But that kind of violence isn't new to me. I've seen it in India at the end of the war. I saw it in Guyana and the Middle East. It was *never* isolated there. Never. We always took it as a sign of something deeper. *Much* deeper, much more *dangerous*.'

'Well certainly,' said Blanshard. 'India, for example. Half the population was starving while the Raj lived like gods . . .'

'Hardly like gods,' snapped Sir Darwin.

'Yes, like gods—by comparison with the native population! They felt deprived for the simple reason that they *were* deprived. I see no comparison whatever between the two situations. It seems to me entirely fatuous, entirely ridiculous, to suggest that a large section of the population of this country is deprived—in the Indian sense, or any other. Macmillan's pronouncement in the late 50s that we'd "never had it so good" was politically inept perhaps, but it was equally true.'

'If I can say a word, sir, on this?' said Robert Paine, the PM's Second Secretary. 'If we're looking for a pattern we shouldn't ignore the fact that Wembley was an open clash between the North and the South. There's a feeling up there of being—out on a limb, you might say.'

'Pure hypothesis,' said Blanshard, turning his chair at an angle to the table.

'Precisely what I'm looking for,' said the PM.

'A little more than pure hypothesis,' continued Paine. He

turned over one or two papers in front of him on the desk. 'In January, you remember, Newcastle and Hull dockers refused to join London in a strike. In the same month, fitters in the Chrysler factory at Liverpool refused a plea from their London executive not to strike. In both cases the issue was trivial. In both cases it was said that decisions made in London had no authority for the North. Only last month you'll remember, workers in five major towns of the North withdrew from membership of the Transport and General Workers' Union on similar grounds. That's the pattern I see. As a Northerner, I wish it wasn't.'

'It's worth exploring,' said the PM. 'I want you to go up and talk to the Northern Development Council. Find out what the grievances are.'

'Perhaps if you went yourself, sir?'

The PM was silent for a moment. Clouds of tobacco smoke wreathed his face and head, as he stared at the picture of Disraeli opposite. 'I think not,' he said at last. 'We don't want to give them the impression of attaching too much importance to this idea.'

It was an unfortunate decision.

It was obvious from the reply to Blackett's request for an interview, that the Minister regarded the refusal of a grant as being a matter of extreme triviality. Blackett was convinced in fact that his letter had not even reached the Minister. The reply was written by, in Blackett's words, 'some minion or other'. It said:

'I have been instructed by the Minister to inform you that he is unable to grant your request for an interview in connection with your theatre building proposals.

'Whilst being most anxious to give his full support to developments in the arts, the Minister must remain aware of the general economic situation and allocate the funds available to him on a system of strict priorities.

'The Minister is aware that from time to time cases will arise with such special features as to justify a deviation from this general policy. The case of the High Wycombe grant to which you refer, contained a number of such special features. In the Minister's view, no such features arise in the case of your own Committee's proposals.'

The Northern Development Council, which Paine was now instructed to visit, had been created during the economic troubles in the North-east in the sixties. It was in effect a toothless standing committee with the vaguest terms of reference, responsible direct to the Minister of Planning. It was charged with 'informing the Minister on the economic and cultural environment in the counties of Northumberland, Cumberland, Westmoreland, Durham, Yorkshire and Lancashire.' It was empowered to 'make recommendations'. Appointments to the Council were made by the Minister on the advice of the Council itself. The Minister had the power to dismiss any member and appoint a replacement, without reference to the Council. At that time, no Minister had ever exercised that right.

The council began its work with vigour and enthusiasm. Its membership of 50 was drawn from industry, commerce, education and the arts throughout the North. It set up subcommittees and working parties to examine the whole Northern scene. Since the central fund allocated to it was inadqeuate even for paying necessary office staff, it financed its research and the publication of its findings from funds contributed by Northern business. It seemed after the first few months of its existence, to be an admirable organization. Initially, even the Minister himself saw it as such.

But, as with all organisms, it began to grow in a way that had not been foreseen by its initiators. It had been brought into being as a means of containing the unrest in the North. Instead, it became a rallying point for the area, canalising feelings and aspirations that had previously been mere subterranean rumblings. As it grew in stature and authority, it clamoured for autonomy and power. It ceased to find satisfaction in making recommendations to the Minister, when it became clear that few of them came to anything. It wanted executive power, the power to implement its own recommendations. There was little that could be done to check its development. No financial pressures could be put on it. The very shortage of central funds which had hampered it initially, had driven it to become financially independent. It could be formally dissolved, but that would not necessarily guarantee its dissolution. It could, conceivably, be declared an illegal organization, but no government dare have taken such a step as long as it was so effectively identified with the Northern spirit.

A month before the visit of Paine, the PM's second secretary, it had formed a small executive body under the somewhat romantic and clandestine title of the Central Committee. The function this Committee was seen at first as the handling of the day to day matters on the Council. It was to this Committee that Blackett, as a founder-member of the Northern Development Council, took his theatre building project after his case had been rejected by Whitehall.

Paine had been a bomber pilot during the war. He flew 58 missions over enemy territory before being hit by 88 mm. fire. His right leg was so badly damaged that it looked at one time as if it would have to be amputated above the knee. First-class surgery and more than a year's devoted nursing and physiotherapy saved it, as far as it could be saved. Even so, he needed a stick to help him walk on it.

He left the service in 1945 at the age of 24. He had had a year's administrative experience as an adjutant. He was a Squadron Leader with a DFC and bar and a DFM. He took up his job again in the Civil Service, but moved within two years into full-time Union work. He liked Union work. He liked the patient negotiation, the careful planning of tactics, the preparing of a well-documented case. His work and approach were never spectacular, never dramatic. But they were sound, methodical and utterly reliable. As he grew in administrative stature, his facts and figures were never questioned. If he stated a fact, then he had researched it thoroughly. Challenged on it, he could quote source, document, page and on occasions even line, to substantiate what he was saying. It was inevitable that he would be noticed in political circles. It was simply a question of time.

Time certainly did elapse. Not until three months after the General Election was Paine invited to take the position of Second Secretary, to work immediately under the Prime Minister's personal direction. The delay had nothing to do with Paine directly. The PM wanted a man who could undertake detailed, laborious negotiations on his behalf. He wanted a man willing to pursue such negotiations to the very end. He wanted a man experienced in finding the facts buried beneath a mound of paper and talk and half-truths and vested interest. Paine was certainly the man for this. Such activity was part of his very nature. But the PM wanted, too, a man who would never reach the limelight in any way, a man whom journalists and photographers and TV cameramen would pass in the street and never notice. And here there was the question of Paine's wife.

Paine's marriage to Valerie Decker was regarded by everyone who knew them at the time, as the most incongruous match possible. To begin with, she was twelve years younger than Paine. She came from a class of society with which he had almost no contact, a class that represented the moneyed establishment, and the Southern establishment at that. Her father, Sir Benjamin Decker, was given a knighthood for 'services to industry' the year before his daughter married. He was one of those successful London businessmen who never appear in the Press, are never recognized in the street—if indeed they ever appear in the street—and whose empire is never defined. Even now, all that can definitely be said of him is that he had substantial property interests in north London, owned a group of moderate-sized stores with branches mainly in the North, and was a governor of one of the more eminent London theatre schools.

His connection with the theatre school is important, for when the question of a finishing school for his daughter arose, he allowed her to persuade him to let her go to the theatre school instead. A friend who was at Benenden with her, clearly remembers her saying: 'I really had to persuade Daddy. He wasn't at all keen on the idea. He wanted me to go to a place near Montreux, but I want to get into the middle of things.'

There is little doubt that the training she received at the school was a help to her, though she never had any intention of going into the profession. It gave her a wide circle of friends and acquaintances, with varying degrees of artistic ability. It turned her from a rather gauche, brash adolescent, into a poised and socially highly competent young woman. She was beautiful, she could dress, she could speak, she could establish immediate and easy relationships with people.

What it was in Paine that attracted her, it is impossible to say. He was 37 at the time, tall and thin—almost cadaverous. He was quiet and withdrawn. He had no sense of dress, no panache. He was awkward in his movements, even discounting his disability. He had no trace of social grace. She said to her matron-of-honour, a week before the marriage: 'I don't love him, of course. I've never loved anyone. But there's a distinct attraction about him. He's so different from anyone I've ever known. I shall enjoy teasing him. I might even turn him into a man—who knows?'

In many ways the marriage was disastrous, and yet it never broke up. Mrs. Paine would disappear for weeks and then make the front page of every national paper. She had appeared again dramatically on a yacht in Cannes, or poised in front of the Schloss at Heidelberg, or shooting grouse in Scotland. Inevitably she was pictured with some new male companion. Outwardly at least, Paine seemed able to endure these episodes. Oddly, they seemed to attract very little publicity to him personally. But they naturally added to the instinctive caution of a political figure like the PM.

It was partly the reservation that the PM had about Paine that made him wait four days after the meeting on May 13th, before writing to the chairman of the Northern Development Council suggesting the visit by his Second Secretary. By that time, matters had passed the point of no return.

The Central Committee of the Northern Development Council, met in Darlington on May 19th. One of the points it chose to consider was Blackett's theatre project, but the principal matter before the meeting was the Prime Minister's letter that had reached the chairman on the 18th. Of the two issues, it appears in perspective that Blackett's was far the more important. The Committee decided that the Minister's decision to withhold a grant, whilst awarding one in the High Wycombe case, was no less than discrimination against a Northern project. It decided unanimously, and after surprisingly little discussion, to override the Minister's decision and to support the project from Northern Development Council funds. If one single decision can be pointed to as being directly responsible for the events of that summer, it is this one. It is crucial to remember that the funds granted by the Central Committee to Blackett, were not private funds. They were public funds, in the sense that they had been contributed indirectly by millions of people in the North to the Northern Development Council. When the Central Committee took upon itself the right to allocate such funds to a Northern project, in defiance of a decision already made by the Minister of Planning, it was in effect challenging the right of the London government to make decisions for the North.

Blackett, who was at the meeting to speak to his proposals, wrote in his diary that night: 'I'm delighted at the decision. It was entirely right. For the first time since the conquest of Danelagh, we have a body that can not only speak for the North, but is prepared to act on its behalf. I had the feeling this afternoon that it is prepared to follow the consequences of its action wherever they may lead. One thing I am quite clear about: the decision of the Central Committee was not based on any short-term vision. This was no irresponsible action. All the full and momentous implications of their actions were seen by members of the Committee. They saw the challenge to the central government and they were prepared to back it to the hilt. If necessary, with their blood, and that of their supporters.'

The Darlington meeting of the Central Committee had done two things. It had defined as the leaders of the North, the five members of the Central Committee. At the same time, it had doomed Paine's mission to failure by crystalizing demands which it was far outside his brief to negotiate.

He left King's Cross on the 5 o'clock Pullman, on Tuesday, May 22nd, and worked throughout the journey. From time to time he consulted his secretary on a point in one of the papers on the table in front of him. Mostly he worked steadily in silence.

Colonel Douglas Fitzwallace of the Central Committee, met them at the barrier in York and walked with them to the Royal Station Hotel on the opposite side of the road. It was a few minutes before 8 p.m. The evening was clear, fresh and cloudless. The air was touched with the perfume of spring blossom. A few late daffodils still bloomed on the grass slopes below the medieval wall. Bells boomed and tinkled the hour as they reached the hotel steps. Paine, though a Northerner by birth, had no sense of being back home. The whole atmosphere was foreign to him, after so long in London. The medieval town, confined within its high, grey-white walls, had nothing in common with the spread and diversity of London. It was not the size that struck him as accounting for the difference, but rather the spirit, the ethos. This was a town drawing itself together for a new role.

When Paine came down from his room into the central lounge, Fitzwallace was waiting for him at a table. Jane Ashe, Paine's secretary, was already with Fitzwallace. Fitzwallace, his monocle glinting as his head moved, was tapping his fingers gently on her forearm as it lay on the table. Paine stood on the stairs for a moment, leaning heavily on his stick and watching them. He felt a touch of jealousy. Fitzwallace looked socially so very competent, Paine felt a little inadequate. He was tired, but that he put down to the journey. Fitzwallace turned and caught sight of him. He said something to Miss Ashe that made her laugh, then sprang to his feet and strode over to Paine.

'Ah, there you are,' said Fitzwallace. 'Let me give you a hand.'

'I'm all right, thank you,' said Paine. He had already taken a dislike to Fitzwallace.

'I see you've brought your briefcase,' said Fitzwallace as they walked over to join Miss Ashe. 'Top secrets, no doubt?'

'I thought we could cover some preliminaries this evening,' said Paine.

33

'Surely not,' said Fitzwallace, opening his eyes so that his monocle fell dramatically and dangled glittering on the end of a black ribbon. 'What do you say, Miss Ashe? Surely not work this evening after all that tiring travel? I thought we would make it a purely social occasion. Dinner here—that seems the best thing. And then perhaps you'd like to have a glance at the town—or a pub maybe. Now be honest, Miss Ashe; doesn't that strike you as being a much better idea than poring over papers and checking terms of reference and seeing if we have any kind of common ground from which we can negotiate?'

'I can't negotiate,' said Paine. 'I can only ask questions and report back.'

'Well there you are,' said Fitzwallace, turning back to Miss Ashe with a sweep of his arms. 'If we can't negotiate, there's nothing further to prevent our enjoying ourselves.'

He took her elbow and she stood up. Paine limped after them into the dining room. As they sat down Fitzwallace said: 'And Valerie—how is she?'

'Valerie?' said Paine, as if he had not heard the name before.

'Your wife; Mrs. Paine,' said Fitzwallace, curling a finger in the direction of the head waiter.

'Oh, I see,' said Paine. 'She's well. You know her, I take it?'

'We're old friends,' said Fitzwallace. 'Alas, it's some years since we saw one another, though I follow her career in the newspapers with mounting admiration. You must be very proud to have so widely travelled and beautiful a woman by your side, so to speak.'

'She's a great—comfort,' said Paine.

Fitzwallace had two images that coalesced in him. He was, on the one hand, everything that the popular image of the English Colonel demands. Tall, perfectly proportioned, upright in carriage, authoritative. On the other hand, there was more than a touch of the poseur about him. His speech and gestures were at times highly dramatic. He was articulate beyond the requirements of a soldier, and highly skilled socially. His use of the monocle suggested a sense more of dramatic than medical necessity. His clothes—fine tailored suit of light-weight tweed, regimental tie, black half-boots—were clearly expensive, and he wore them in a way that drew attention to the fact. There

34

was nothing about him that fitted the popular Southern image of the Northerner. Paine was uneasy in his company. He felt that behind the charm and ease, rested a force that was savage, unscrupulous and destructive.

'You see, you don't understand us in London,' Fitzwallace was saying. 'Now take myself, for example. Miss Ashe here probably regards me as an illiterate boor, simply because I come from the North . . .'

'Oh, please . . .' said Miss Ashe.

'No, of course. You're much too well brought up to admit it. And of course too kind. It must be a great comfort to you Paine, to have someone so extremely attractive to lean on in times of stress.'

'Miss Ashe is most efficient,' said Paine. He wondered if Fitzwallace was making a veiled reference to his leg.

'Efficient? Yes of course. How else could a young and beautiful woman reach a position of such responsibility? You see, I am now fifty,' he said, returning to his earlier theme, 'officially retired. But I'm not a vegetable. I don't sit in an armchair all day and brood on the past. Not a bit of it. I take part in all kinds of activities: committees of one sort or another, sport, the stock market, politics—in a very parochial sense . . . You know? Now: I would say I was a fairly typical product of the North. We really don't eat our young, you know. Not all of us. We let them grow up. They produce the wealth for you in the South.'

'I'm a Northerner myself,' said Paine.

'By birth,' said Fitzwallace quickly. 'Yes I know. I looked you up. Middlesbrough. Depressing place. You're a shade older than I am,' he said, with a glance at Miss Ashe, 'and I wouldn't have thought you'd worn quite so well.'

After dinner, they took coffee in the lounge. At last, Paine looked at his watch. 'I think if you'll excuse me . . .' he said.

'It's not really a question of birth,' said Fitzwallace. 'You've lived most of your life out of the North, now admit it. London, I'm sure you'll agree, has some corrupting influence on you— the easy life, *la dolce vita*? No; I see none of that essential quality of the North in you—not any longer, I'm afraid.' He adjusted his monocle and stared at Paine.

'Perhaps not,' said Paine. His leg was aching badly. He wanted to go to bed. 'How would you define it, this "essential quality of the North"?'

'Hm.' said Fitzwallace, leaning back and pressing the palms of his hands together. 'A certain arrogance. Defiance, perhaps. But hidden—subterranean. You need to look for it.'

'Where?'

'In the eyes,' said Fitzwallace.

The meeting the next morning, known now as the York Meeting, was certainly an historic one. But it was not memorable in the sense that vital decisions were made at it. Nor was it memorable for its length. It lasted, in fact, for less than 30 minutes.

Paine knew, as he sat down facing Sir Brian Wordsworth, that the decisions had already been made. This group of five men had already thrashed out their position. There was nothing for him to do but listen.

Wordsworth made a preliminary statement. Paine could feel the authority of the man as he spoke. He talked of 'long-standing injustices'. He quoted briefly from figures before him, the comparative sums spent in the North and in the South-east on hospitals, schools and housing. 'You were a Northerner,' he said. 'You know the truth of what I'm saying. For two hundred years we have been a depressed race. We still live in conditions that are a scandal in any country claiming to be civilized— conditions in which no Southerner would keep his dog. We've produced the wealth of this country and it's been stolen from us. But we're going no further with you. This is where slavery ends.'

He turned to the four others. Each said a few words in support of their chairman's statement. All looked unshakably determined. When Paine was asked to comment he had nothing to say. He was acutely aware that London had mistimed every thing. The PM should have come himself and he should have moved much earlier. Paine knew that he was the wrong man to face such a meeting.

'Very well,' said Wordsworth, when his colleagues had finished speaking. 'This is what you will tell the Prime Minister.' He opened a file and took out a piece of paper. It had been signed by a number of people. 'Point 1,' Wordsworth read. 'That the six Northern counties of Cumberland, Westmorland, Lancashire, Northumberland, Durham and Yorkshire, shall be designated in future as "The North". Point 2: That the City of York, as the ancient capital of the North, shall be given the status of the second city in England. Point 3: That the Northern Development Council be redesignated The Council of the North. Point 4: That the Central Committee of the Northern Development Council, all five members of which are present this morning, shall become the executive body of the Council of the North. Point 5: That the Council of the North shall have authority to design and implement its own constitution, without reference to Westminster. Point 6: That, under the final authority of Westminster on matters of foreign policy and the national defence only, the Council of the North shall have power to govern in the North.' He looked up at Paine for a moment, and then passed the paper to him. 'Do we make ourselves quite clear?'

Paine tapped his stick on the carpet. 'Quite clear,' he said. There was nothing else he could say. The points were abundantly clear. So was the intention behind them. The sense of solid unity of the five men who faced him across the long table, made it unnecessary for him to say any more. He simply wanted to get back to London as soon as possible and report the whole incredible proceedings. 'There's just one question, if I might . . .' he said, looking up at Sir Brian Wordsworth.

'Well?' said Wordsworth, his heavy cheeks shaking a little as he spoke.

'It's naturally outside my brief to indicate whether the points you make can be accepted by the Prime Minister or not, as a basis for negotiation . . .'

'Come now, Paine,' said Fitzwallace, polishing his monocle. 'You know damn' well no one in your part of the world could possibly accept them. I mean, you understand them don't you? You know what it is we're asking for?'

'It's not my place to consider the implications,' said Paine. 'I can only report the facts.'

37

'You've come a long way since your Middlesbrough days, Paine, haven't you? They've got you all right, haven't they? You know your place and your terms of reference. Can't you stand up like a man and say what's in your mind?' He screwed the monocle into his eye, and smiled charmingly at Paine.

'You were going to ask a question' said Wordsworth.

'In the event of the Prime Minster's refusing to accept the points you have put forward—er, what is your reaction likely to be?'

Wordsworth leaned back heavily in his chair and let his hands drop on to the arms. He seemed to dismiss the point as trivial. 'We think that our points are reasonable as they stand —reasonable and minimal. We'll negotiate from nothing less. If they're not accepted, then we shall break all contact with London.'

'This of course would be revolution,' said Paine.

'The Prime Minster would call it that no doubt,' agreed Wordsworth. 'But by that time he'd be *your* Prime Minster, not ours.'

'But . . .' said Paine. But again there seemed nothing useful he could say.

'You're wondering, I suppose, if we have the power and authority. Let me state the facts: the Northern Development Council speaks for the North—make no mistake about that. It's not the toothless body that you set up two years ago. And *we* speak for the Council. We've both the power and the authority. Perhaps it's our determination you doubt? In that case you'd better look at the five of us again. Decide for yourself. Then remember that every one of us speaks for two or three million Northerners. And every one of those is on the point of explosion . . . Have I put your mind at rest?'

'Thank you,' said Paine. 'I'm quite clear.'

The membership of the Central Committee at that time is a vital factor in any understanding of subsequent events. Had the membership been other than it was, it is quite possible that the battles of Nottingham and Cricklewood, and the sack of the western approaches to the capital, would not have taken place.

Sir Brian Wordsworth was 58. He was physically impressive, well above middle height, broad shouldered, running now a little to fat. The extra weight he carried showed not only at the waistline, but also in the neck and around the jaw. His hair, thinning only slightly at the temples, losing now its earlier deep brown colour, was kept short. His close-clipped moustache, bristling as he spoke, was turning from red to grey. When he spoke, it was in the accents of the Northern country gentleman, his voice deep, a little gruff and unmelodious.

He was the seventh Baron Wordsworth, with family connections with both the Howards and the Mowbrays. His wife, a little younger than he, had connections with the Percys of Northumberland. His home estate, on the borders of the North and East Ridings of Yorkshire, and running into each, ran to more than fifteen hundred acres of rolling wold land. His house, an eighteenth century gentleman's residence reputedly designed by Vanbrugh at the time he was working on Castle Howard, incorporated the cellars and dungeons of a much earlier castle. His real wealth came from the vast textile interests in the West Riding of Yorkshire, established by his great-grandfather, but he had investments in a wide range of other industry and enterprise throughout the world.

Essentially feudal in outlook, he was deeply concerned about the well-being of his tenant farmers and his staff. At the same time, he would brook no questioning of his authority. Only three years earlier, he had thrown a farmer physically off his land for little more than reminding him that democracy gives a tenant the right to question his landlord's judgement. He was ambitious, but again in the feudal sense, rather than in the modern political sense. If he could have extended his lands by conquest, he would probably have done so. He saw society as a hierarchy, fixed for all time in heaven. His own position in this hierarchy was a little below that of God. He acknowledged allegiance to the Crown, though probably never to Parliament. But that allegiance he saw as an agreement between two powerful members of a fixed elite, an agreement that might be broken on either side. It was never an allegiance of inferior to superior. He was essentially the outdoor, established, Northern landed gentleman. The outdoor showed in the ruddy, rather course texture of his skin, and in the tweeds and cavalry twills he wore. The gentleman showed in the tailoring and in the quality of the cloth. It showed too in the power and aggression of his manner.

Albert Cohen Rubinstein was a Manchester Jew. Born in Cheetham Hill of wealthy parents, he was educated at Manchester Grammar School and Balliol. Always a brilliant and determined worker, he had entered the field of entertainment on the management side in the early days of the talkies, and built an empire of theatres and cinemas by the time he was 35. From then until his early 40s, he had devoted all his time to a study of the rise of the Greek classical civilization following very much in the footsteps of Schliemann. After he had published privately his seven volumes of 'The Fourteen Cities of Troy' and his two volume work, 'The Greek City States: essays in ideal government', he returned to Manchester and was invited to the chairmanship of the Independent Television Company GRANADA, the company controlling ITV programmes for much of the North. It was his intention in doing so, to 'give the North the identity it had never felt'. His ideal would have been to create city states on the Greek lines, of such places as Leeds, Manchester, Liverpool, Newcastle and Hull. But it was sufficient for him at the moment to lend his authority and money to the support of an independent Northern province.

He was 64 and impressive in appearance, with a heavy square-cut greying beard, greying curly hair and rather incongruous pince-nez, which had made a permanent indentation in the bridge of his nose. Large, impressively slow-moving, liberal, humanitarian, European in outlook and interests, he came as close as any man might hope to the ideal of being civilized.

By contrast with Rubinstein, Sidney Olsen looked at first sight quite undistinguished. True, he was a pleasant looking young man, with an open boyish face and dark hair with the suggestion of a wave in it. He was 28, but gave the impression of being perhaps five years younger, partly because of his looks, perhaps more because of the impression he gave of innocent immediacy. Innocent, not in the sense of immaturity, but rather

40

in a total lack of cynicism or world-weariness. He seemed to be totally immersed in the business of living, without in any way being borne down by it. The burning sense of vigour, of boundless idealistic enthusiasm, was what remained in ones memory of him when the image of the boyish face and the ready smile had faded.

He could look back already on a varied career. Born in Newcastle, he left the Royal Grammar School at 16 with five tolerable passes in O level subjects, and a scholastic reputation for laziness. The reputation was not quite justified. What was nearer the truth was that he saw little relevance in academic achievement. More than that, he was frightened by the possibility that concentration on this particular aspect of himself might interfere with the development of other aspects that he sensed were more important. He took up the guitar with great enthusiasm, at a time when most other young men were doing the same. Whilst working in the offices of the National Coal Board during the day, he played with a Group in the clubs during the evenings. But he had explored the possibilities of the guitar very soon, and his enthusiasm ran out, or it turned rather in a new direction.

He succeeded in getting a place at the Royal Academy of Dramatic Art in Gower Street. His enthusiasm was high, but his talent in this particular direction was extremely thin. He was asked to leave at the end of the first term. 'The best advice I can give you, Olsen,' said the Principal, 'is to stay out of the theatre, unless you want to wear a rut in the pavement outside the Labour Exchange.' Nevertheless, he stuck to the theatre for almost two years, stage managing in small repertory theatres, doing insignificant walk-on parts on tour. But the desire to organize, had begun to show itself in him, and that, coupled with his irrepressible enthusiasm, made him something of a nuisance to some of the managements for whom he worked.

He formed his own Group eventually, and toured with it abroad He played the guitar still, and occasionally he did the vocals. The success of the Group was moderately encouraging. But the real significance of the experience for Olsen, was that it convinced him that his strength lay not in performance but in organization. He could organize young talent, he could encourage and enthuse it, he could market it. His meteoric rise to riches and renown is, of course, well known. He discovered and launched *The Harlequins* and the *Five Past Tens*. A dozen other groups of young entertainers claim that any success they have had is entirely because of his management of them. He created the *Tyneside Trend* in entertainment, which so totally eclipsed the *Liverpool Sound*. The *Beatles*, now in retirement in Nepal, said of him recently: 'Brian Epstein breached the wall, but Sid Olsen took over the town.'

At the time of the York Meeting, Sidney Olsen, both personally and through the teams he managed, was almost venerated by millions of young people. He could command fifty divisions of young people with a chord. Yet he seemed surprisingly unaware of the fact. In a television interview he once said: 'Listen: it's not the money I want. I don't need any more of that anyway. It's just I get a kick out of organizing the kids so they show what they've got. And I get a kick out of sticking up two fingers at the entertainment establishment.' Later, he said: 'I see the North like I see young people. Neither's seen much of the sun.'

Sir Felix Brunton represented, in a sense, the other side of the coin. Of middle height, rather thin, a little stooping, he had in repose the face and eyes of some sensitive animal. Earlier in his career as a musician, a garrulous oboe player had given him the nickname of 'Basset hound'. The name stuck, because it had a certain aptness. There was in his face something that suggested a gentle, well-bred animal, trained for a part that it found vaguely distasteful.

Twenty years earlier, he had given up his position with the New York Symphony Orchestra, to take over the Scheller Orchestra in Leeds at the personal invitation of the Earl of Harewood. The orchestra had at that time almost no outside financial support and no permanent building of its own. Ten miles beyond the Leeds boundary, no one but musicians had heard of it. He had worked eighteen hours a day to weld its members into an orchestra and to secure permanent financial backing from outside. Rubenstein was one of the first to give him unstinted financial help and publicity, help that had resulted in a deep and permanent friendship between the two of them.

At the time of the York Meeting, the orchestra was one of the most renowned in Europe, with its own permanent concert hall and rehearsal rooms at the back of the Merrion Centre in the middle of Leeds. It had helped to make that city a centre for music that vied with Rome, London, Paris, Vienna and New York. Sir Felix Brunton himself was almost revered, not only by musicians and music lovers but by thousands of influential people interested in the arts in general. At the age of 52, he was regarded by many as one of the five great conductors of the day.

Yet Paine remembers him as a rather shadowy figure, a man who seemed a little out of place. Not so much out of his depth, as out of his element. 'I gather,' says Paine, looking back on the meeting now, 'that in rehearsal he was little less than a tyrant, with a driving force that was quite irresistible. But I saw no sign of it that morning. What I saw was a rather shadowy person, very soberly dressed and with a certain sadness about the eyes. A brilliant musician no doubt, but not a political leader. I think now that this assessment of him was fairly accurate.'

The fifth member of the Central Committee, was Colonel Douglas Bright Fitzwallace, the second son of a gentleman farmer who had raised a troop of horse from the Yorkshire Wolds for the 1914-18 war. The horse, indeed, was almost a family symbol. It had been so for most of the two-hundred years that the family had held and farmed land. The Fitzwallaces were acknowledged to be amongst the finest of the smaller bloodstock breeders in the country. Over the years, the stud had been used by British royalty and by the wealthy and more enterprising breeders of France and America. The South American breeder, Jose dos Remanos Vermenitac, was in fact staying at the Fitzwallace stable at the time of the York Meeting. Douglas Fitzwallace had broken with the family farming and breeding tradition on the death of his father, when it became obvious to him that if he stayed he would always be subject to the overall direction of his elder brother, Alan. It was not in his nature to accept such a position. It was very much against his mother's wishes that he left Marlborough and went to Sandhurst. His determination to avoid the domination of his brother, caused estrangement from his family. His visits to the estate were rare. Only with his sister Evelyn, did he preserve any permanent relationship.

Fitzwallace was in fact a good deal more complicated than he appeared. A casual acquaintance might easily consider him charming, highly socialized, somewhat superficial. Something of a poseur; a swashbuckling Don Juan. It was really one of his strengths, that he could be so completely misunderstood. It disarmed the opposition, so that when he struck there were no defences raised to parry the blow. It was not generally known that he had an outstanding service record, not in any way indicated by his rank. He was administratively brilliant, though the brilliance was frequently masked behind the aura of the privateer. The War Office had never been entirely sure of him. His methods were unorthodox, though they rarely failed to get him what he wanted. In a condition of permanent war, he would without question have been an outstanding figure. But the condition of prolonged peace found him losing interest in day to day Army routine.

At Marlborough, he was remembered as 'a rather dreamy youth'. At Sandhurst he emerged at the head of his year. Despite his long absences from the North, his professional travels abroad, he never regarded himself as anything but a Northerner, with his traditions and roots in the Yorkshire countryside. At 50, he was still a first-rate horseman. He had in his flat in York, one of the finest private collections of Elizabethan weapons in the country. The secretary of the Arms and Armour Society once said of him: 'I regard Colonel Fitzwallace as probably the finest exponent of authentic rapier play in Europe.' He was a student of the poems of Andrew Marvell, with whom he claimed some distant relationship. In his thirties, he had brought out two small volumes of nature poems under the name of Douglas Bright.

It was Fitzwallace who had brought together the members of the Central Committee. They represented, he felt, much of what seemed to him to be the North—feudalism, land, the Army, the Arts, business, superimposed on a volcanic vigour. He said once to Olsen: 'I should have liked to add a member of the clergy; ideally, a non-Christian member of the Church of

44

England. But such a paragon is hard to find.' Incongruous though he undoubtedly appeared to Paine as a member of any responsible body, he was nonetheless the unifying factor of the Central Committee—almost its *raison d'être.*

There were powerful and vociferous members of the Northern Development Council, not members of the Central Committee, whose influence on the five members of the Committee at this time, cannot be ignored. Two such members are of particular importance. Stephen Jackman, tall, gaunt, anxious about developments that he saw were slipping rapidly out of the control of the Northern Development Council as a whole, sent a stream of memoranda to all members of the Central Committee from the privacy of his study in the University. Dr. Colin Blackett, far more politically astute than Jackman and unencumbered by any of his classical ideals, exerted his influence on the Committee exclusively through Colonel Fitzwallace.

Paine took a taxi to Downing Street and the diplomatic car out to Chequers. He got there at 9.30 p.m. The PM was chairing the Siamese Committee and he had given the strictest instructions not to be disturbed. Paine settled himself into a chair in the upstairs committee room, where the ferocious figure of Churchill glowered down at him from the wall opposite the balcony window. From the chair he could see the lawns and the parkland beyond. He felt it must be the last peaceful summer evening the place would see.

It was a little after midnight when the PM himself came in. He looked tired and drawn. The puffed flesh beneath his eyes was more pronounced. His clothes smelled strongly of tobacco smoke. 'Well?' was all he said.

Paine handed him the document that Wordsworth had given him. He sat down on the corner of a chair. When he had read it he put it on the table beside him and said: 'How serious are they?'

'I think entirely serious,' said Paine.

'They must know that this is ridiculous—absolutely impossible?'

'I think so,' said Paine.

'Then they want an open breach, is that it?'

'They seem prepared for it, sir,' said Paine.

'Very well,' said the PM getting up. 'They leave me no choice. Get back to London and issue orders for their arrest. I want the five of them brought here . . . No. I'll make an example of them. Take them to the Tower.'

Paine issued the necessary instructions in the early hours of the morning. But the plans of the Central Committee had been extremely thorough. By noon it became clear to Paine that the instructions to the police in the Northern areas had either miscarried or were being deliberately ignored.

3

WORDSWORTH was aware of the attempt of London to have him and the rest of the Central Committee arrested, through the channels that had been built up during the previous months. It remained to be seen whether the military elements in the North would remain as united as the police, when pressure was put on them. When, by May 26th, no reply had been received from the PM regarding the document that had been handed to Paine, the Central Committee decided to publish the principal points in the document and declare a *de facto* acceptance of them by London. They chose to do this through an announcement called *The Declaration of Separateness* on the Northern independent television networks and through the 'pirate' radio ship, Radio 38, which lay off Scarborough. The *Declaration* was paid for as an advertisement. Wordsworth presented the case on radio and Sidney Olsen on television. The broadcasts covered these points:

> That the Northern Development Council considered that the North could no longer be effectively governed from London.
>
> That the Northern Development Council had been redesignated The Council of the North. As such it was responsible for the government of the North, with its headquarters in the City of York.
>
> That in the counties of Cumberland, Westmorland, Lancashire, Northumberland, Durham and Yorkshire, all monies that had in the past been paid direct to the central government would be payable to the Council of the North in York.

The broadcasts were followed by a vigorous, rousing new tune sung by the *Harlequins*, that had been commissioned by Sidney

47

Olsen as long ago as early February. Periodic repetitions of the broadcasts took place throughout the day, and the new tune— 'Free to Live'—was heard at half-hour intervals.

That evening, the Scheller Orchestra, under Sir Felix Brunton, gave a concert of revolutionary music in support of the Council of the North. Afterwards, Sir Felix made the most outspoken public statement of his career in support of autonomy for the North. He went, in fact, beyond the public statements that had been put out on radio and television, though not beyond the spirit of them.

In Liverpool, Manchester and Newcastle, Olsen organized popular concerts for teenagers at which his most celebrated groups appeared. Enthusiasm for the new development was overwhelming. Olsen said afterwards: 'I've seen the receptions the Groups used to get in the old days. Police everywhere, trying to keep the kids in order. But they were nothing to what I saw in Newcastle that night. They weren't out of control, you understand. They marched in very good order down Pilgrim Street and over Tyne Bridge into Gateshead. But the power there, the enthusiasm! You'd have thought they'd just broken out of gaol. It must have been like that in the early days of the French Revolution, or the start of the American Revolution. It was the same that night at all our concerts.'

In Manchester, Leeds, Bradford and Hull, university students, students from the Colleges of Education, the Schools of Art, the Colleges of Technology, and in some cases the schools, marched through the towns with banners shouting their support and breaking into the chorus of the new song 'Free to Live'. In the University of York, with its larger numbers of students from the South, there was some limited violence. A counter-march by Southern students down Tower Street and Clifford Street, was broken up in Nessgate by students from the Technical College and from St. John's College of Education. A girl student from East Finchley was almost drowned by being suspended head down in a bucket of beer in the Three Tuns in Coppergate. Two men students from Brighton were thrown into the river from Ouse Bridge.

One of the minor incidents that took place that day, passed almost unnoticed in the general clamour. Yet it had implications for the Council of the North and the whole liberation movement that had not been foreseen. A group of foreign students from the Dept. of Textiles in the University of Leeds, marched down Briggate carrying a banner which read: 'Liberation for the North'. The group was made up of four Nigerians, two Ghanaians and a Zambian. People who saw them pushing through the traffic, were amused. They thought it incongruous to see coloured students in active sympathy with the North. But Colonel Fitzwallace, when he heard of the incident, was quick to see its significance. 'We've taken too parochial a view of things,' he told Wordsworth the next morning. 'We've seen this as the liberation of one part of England from the domination of another. You know, it's nothing of the sort. It's part of a world liberation movement. No wonder we have African sympathizers. We're doing no less than they did some years ago—demanding independence from a central body on which we have no real representation and with which we have nothing in common.'

'Yes,' said Wordsworth, dismissively. He had already sensed the truth of this, but he had no interest in world movements except in so far as they might be harnessed to further his own aims. 'You'd better look at these. Encouraging, I think. They came in during the night and earlier this morning.' He passed a bundle of papers to Fitzwallace. Some were telegrams, most were telephone messages.

A telegram from the Lord Mayor of Nottingham read: EVERY SYMPATHY WITH YOUR ENDEAVOURS STOP GREATLY DISTURBED THAT THIS CITY AND COUNTY NOT INCLUDED IN DEFINITION OF NORTH STOP URGENTLY REQUEST CONSULTATION WITH YOU WITH VIEW TO FORMAL IDENTIFICATION WITH YOUR MOVEMENT.

A telegram from the authorities in Chester ran on very much the same lines. A message from Derby, on behalf of the City and County of Derby, received by telephone at 1.32 in the morning said: 'We are all extremely interested in and sympathetic towards the creation of the Council of the North. We offer you any support you may require from us, though we cannot at this stage ask for any formal association with you.

We should be very glad if you would keep us informed of all developments.'

There were three offers of support from Scotland. An offer of support from Wales was given in the most militant terms: 'To our comrades in the North, we offer all support possible, in their fight against the crippling domination of the English. Should the time come when physical support is needed, we shall offer such support unflinchingly.'

'Well,' said Fitzwallace. 'What do they mean, do you think, by "the English"?' He twirled his monocle on the end of its ribbon. 'It looks as if we were unnecessarily cautious. It seems that we have the whole country behind us.'

'Hardly the whole country,' said Wordsworth. 'In any case, that doesn't matter. The question now is how how far we have the North behind us.'

It was, of course, the vital question.

It was a day of intense activity, a day of telephone calls, telegrams, memoranda and personal visits. Whitehall spent the morning trying to find out exactly what had happened and the extent to which the Council of the North constituted a genuine threat to the security of the State. The PM flew north just after 10 a.m., but had to return after being refused permission to land at both Ringway and Yeadon. By lunchtime, it was obvious in London that the Northern threat was real enough.

The afternoon was spent in securing the support of Members for a declaration of a State of National Emergency. At 4.15 p.m. the PM drove to Windsor to see the Queen. He was back in London just before 7 p.m. At the House he learned that it was just possible that Parliament would approve powers under a National Emergency. Many MPs were extremely confused and undecided. But in the absence of any real information, and in view of the transcripts of the Northern television and radio broadcasts that had been circulated amongst them, it was predicted that there would be a majority of about 10. A little before midnight, a State of National Emergency was declared. The majority in the House was, in fact, 7.

The PM acted at once under his barely gained emergency powers. At 2 a.m. on the 28th, a detachment of Household Cavalry left Wellington Barracks in a 3-ton army lorry. They had been carefully selected and briefed. Not one of them had been born north of Barnet. Ensign Davidson, in command, was a native of Guildford. Their task was to arrest the five members of the Central Committee and return with them to the Tower.

Davidson remembers that morning as clear and bright. They drove along M1 at an average of 40 m.p.h. He would have moved more quickly, but all the men had been pulled out of their beds and it seemed essential to him that they should get some sleep. At speeds above 40, the vehicle rolled too much for sleep to be possible. At 5 a.m. it was fully light. They were approaching the boundary of south Nottinghamshire. The woods shone, dark and dewy, in the clear light. In the far distance ahead, the black backbone of a slag-heap stood sharply against the northern sky.

A little before 6 a.m. Davidson instructed the driver to pull off the motorway. There, amongst the remaining trees of Sherwood Forest, they had breakfast. There were twenty of them, mostly under 22 years old. They stretched and yawned and rubbed their eyes. One damped his hand on the heavily-dewed grass and wiped his face. A few were clutching light automatic weapons, but most had left their equipment in the lorry. Most of them began at last to drop down on groundsheets they had laid on the grass. They had heard that there was trouble in the North. Few knew what it amounted to. Only three had ever been north of Hertfordshire before, and those three seemed only to remember the grim streets, the rain and the cold. Corporal Harrison, a Lance Corporal of Horse until the *Army Act of Rationalisation of Nomenclature* the previous year had standardised the rank of all non-commissioned officers and men, had a grandmother in Skipton. All he said as he looked around at the early morning scene was: 'Jesus Christ!'

Watkin, who had driven through the night, leaned back against one of the front wheels of the lorry and closed his eyes.

Davidson, a mug of tea in one hand, moved about amongst his troops. It was his first experience of action. He wanted to make sure that he came out of it creditably. 'All right,' he said at last, taking up a position between the men and the small portable cooking stove. 'You've probably gathered what we're up against. These bastards are in revolt. Now there are only five of them. It's our job to get hold of them and take them back to town. Nothing difficult about that, so long as everyone obeys orders.'

'The bloody pratt,' muttered Corporal Harrison, pulling his beret down to his eyebrows. He had seen action in Sarawak. He was in that last bomb-throwing incident in Aden when four of his patrol had been killed.

A more experienced officer would have had Harrison on his ear for the remark. Davidson, who hadn't quite made out the words, chose to ignore it. He took two maps from his pocket and spread them on the bonnet of the lorry. 'All right you men.' he said. 'Gather round so you can all see.'

They grouped round the lorry, but only a few of them could actually see the maps. One was a general map of the area. The other a detailed map of the City of York, with various buildings marked in red crayon.

'This,' said Davidson, pointing with a cane, 'is the way in: Doncaster by-pass then A1 just beyond Ferrybridge. There's a pub here—the Brotherton Fox—and from there we're making for Tadcaster. Tadcaster we hit A64. Dual carriageway then, all the way into York. Got it?'

There were grunts from some of the nearer men. They might have meant anything.

'Right,' said Davidson. He folded up the map and drew forward the other. 'Now we come into the town here . . . Blossom Street. Good wide road. Should give us no trouble. There's a wall here . . .'

'Wall, sir?' said Watkin, still drowsy from lack of sleep.

'There's a wall round the old city, according to the map. You'll have to watch it here . . . There's an archway, but it's no more than seven feet wide. You manage that all right, Watkin?'

'Sir,' said Watkin.

'The house is down the hill here: number 55, right hand side. Immediately beyond, a turn on the right—park down there. But it's narrow, Watkin, remember that.'

'Sir.'

'Sounds like raiding a bloody museum,' grumbled Corporal Harrison.

'That's enough, Corporal Harrison.'

'Sir.'

'Watkin, you'll stay in the driving seat. Don't go to sleep. Sergeant Benbow, detail four men to stay inside the lorry.'

Benbow still found it difficult to accustom himself to the new title of *Sergeant*, after so many years as *Corporal of Horse*. 'That'll be you Smith, you Bellinger—Drake and Evans,' he said, jabbing his finger towards them.

'When we get inside, take four men and look through the cellars and ground floor rooms.'

'Cellars, sir?' said Benbow.

'There may not be any—just in case. Then Corporal Harrison and four men take the first floor. The rest follow me to the top. You know the men we're after Sergeant?'

'Sir.'

'Corporal Harrison?'

'Sir,' said Harrison wearily.

'Wake up Corporal Harrison, for God's sake,' muttered Benbow. 'If this was action, you'd get the bloody lot of us done in.'

'When you've got them, shove 'em into the lorry as quick as you can. We don't want any trouble if it can be avoided. When I give the word, Watkin, pull away. First right, by the look of it, then right again. Left at the T-junction and you're back on the hill facing out of town. Never mind the details now; I'll be in the cab with you . . . Now are you all clear?'

There were nods and grunts from the men. 'Clear, sir,' said Watkin.

'Good,' said Davidson, folding up the city map. 'Better detail the men to stay with you, Sergeant—and those to go with Corporal Harrison.'

'Right,' said Sergeant Benbow. 'Stand up now and let's have a look at you. Now then, with me—Wilk, Dewey, Stoner . . .'

'Take your time, Sergeant,' said Davidson quietly. 'Can't leave here before 8.30 or we'll find the place empty. Want to catch them redhanded, as it were. If the men want to get their heads down for a couple of hours, let them. They must be fresh if we're to preserve the element of surprise.'

Fitzwallace was in his flat. The lounge was a large, rectangular room, the ceiling decorated with plaster motifs. Bookcases had been built into the alcoves on either side of the wide fireplace. Four swords, placed upright, decorated the chimney breast. On the wall opposite, a series of framed plates from Angelo's *Ecole des Armes* hung in a diagonal line. A large, oak-framed grandfather clock, ticked slowly from the far corner. It was a minute after 2 a.m.

Olsen was sitting on the edge of a deep leather armchair, his face shining in the light of the large standard lamp by the window. 'But what are we, we Northerners?' he was saying, his hands thrown out towards Fitzwallace. 'Where do our roots go down? Where's our real home? Are we Scandinavians, really? They say we use plenty of words in common with them.' Even the lateness of the hour had no dampening effect on his enthusiasm. Fitzwallace smiled, leaning back deeply into his chair. 'I went to Copenhagen two years ago,' said Olsen. 'Fixing up a concert for *The Harlequins*. They were just getting known then. You know *Tivoli*—that entertainers' fairyland in the very middle of the town?'

'I know it,' said Fitzwallace.

'Walking through all the shows there—magicians, acrobats, sword-swallowers, dancers, musicians, you know—I came across this flea circus. I'd heard about them, of course. Fascinating idea! But I'd never seen one. Do you know what they called it in Danish? *Lope Circus!* There you are—*lope*.' He pronounced it *loppa*. 'Willie Brunell of ATV was with me. It meant nothing to him. But *lop*—well I was brought up with that word. "Fit as a *lop*", "A bedful of *lops*". Do you know, it wasn't till I got to school that I heard the word *flea*? And don't they say the dialect on the coast here's very like Scandinavian?'

'I've heard it said,' said Fitzwallace, twirling the brandy in his glass and admiring the shine on the toes of his black boots, 'that a Dane can understand the dialect of Flamborough. But it's all damned nonsense.'

'But we've connections?'

'We've connections of course. Nobody would deny it. Longboats, no doubt, still buried in the sands off the coast, if we chose to look for them. Blood of the old Vikings still soaked into the earth. That old Norse king—seven straight foot of him—cut down and still rotting at Stamford Bridge. By God . . . ' he pulled himself upright in his chair, suddenly furious. 'Do you know what really gave me the clearest insight into their attitude? You remember the nine-hundredth anniversary of Hastings and Stamford Bridge—1966 it was? For Hastings, the Post Office were issuing a commemorative stamp. We pressed for a stamp to commemorate Stamford Bridge. Did they take any notice? Not a bit of it. "Not of sufficient national importance", they told us. "What do you think would happen if we issued a stamp in commemoration of every event in British history?" Three months later they issued a stamp of the Sussex countryside! What's the significance of that to a Northerner? That damn' fool Harold Godwinson—what kind of a king is it who lets himself be shot with an arrow in the eye? And that giant Hardrada—red-headed, deep-throated, he must have been. Royal. Cut down and walked over in that swampy ground. And we're not even allowed to remember him on a damn' postage stamp. To destroy the identity of a people, first destroy their mythology. Do you know what Stamford Bridge means to them—apart from a dangerous rallying point for the North? It means Chelsea playing at home! But make no mistake about it, Sidney. I can hear the bone-biters and brain-crushers being taken out of the outhouses from here to the northern border. We'll live to see the trolls raping that luscious Sussex countryside.'

He got up and walked about the room, twirling his monocle. Despite the late hour, he seemed too excited to stay in his chair.

'I envy you,' said Olsen. 'The issue's clearer to you than it is to me. I have this—well this force, this drive and energy . . . I'm burning. I want to direct it. Things move so quickly . . . '

He got up and put both hands on the mantelpiece and stared down into the empty hearth. 'I should so like to do something of value.' he said. 'Something—entirely worthwhile.'

'Yes,' said Fitzwallace, as if he were not really listening any more. He had gone to the window and drawn open the curtains. The night was clear and lovely. A barge was snuffling past on the river outside. 'Action is the only worthwhile condition of man. But there's nothing at all for us to do now. We must wait. The next move is theirs, not ours.' He turned away from the window at last, and sat down again. 'You know,' he said suddenly, 'I wish we had someone else in the chair.'

'Not Wordsworth, you think?'

'A born leader, I admit—of a kind. But it's not the right kind. Feudalism isn't the answer any more. People don't respond to that kind of hierarchy now. He'd have us all in chains if he could, or playing mummers round his table. It's not liberation for the North he's after. He wants liberation for Wordsworth—to do as he damn' well likes. I wonder where we'll end up with him.'

When the phone rang, it took him a moment to realize what the noise was that suddenly shattered the peace of the room.

'Shall I . . . ?' said Olsen, lifting his head from the mantelpiece.

'No', said Fitzwallace. 'No, I'll get it . . . Who?' he said, into the phone. 'I see . . . No, go on . . .'

There was a long silence whilst the caller spoke. Olsen turned and leaned his back against the mantelpiece. He looked at the odd bachelor decoration of the room.

'Very well,' said Fitzwallace at last. 'Keep in touch with me.'

He put down the phone slowly. He looked totally preoccupied with what had been said to him. He took up his brandy again and drank it. At last he put down his glass and slapped Olsen on the shoulder. 'That was a contact in London,' he said. 'They've made the next step. A detachment left Wellington Barracks half an hour ago. We're to be arrested and taken to the Tower. Personal instructions of the Prime Minister. Now isn't that honour and glory for us. I'd never have believed that damn' little upstart had it in him! Come, Sidney: we must get ready to welcome these chaps.'

The element of surprise that Ensign Davidson had spoken of, would certainly be there. But he was not to be the engineer of it.

The lorry pulled through the narrow arch of Micklegate Bar and into the medieval city of York, a little before 10 that bright morning. Davidson remembers being surprised at the lightness of the traffic. A motor cycle roared past on its way out of the city. Two men with rolls of fishing equipment, turned from the window of Spelman's bookshop and watched them as they approached. But there was only one other vehicle in sight, an old black furniture van parked on the left of the road outside the Adelphi Hotel.

'Watch it,' said Davidson. 'That's the place on your right. You want this turning here. St. Martin's Lane.'

Watkin slowed down and began to turn the wheel. 'One-way street, sir,' he said, putting his foot on the brake.

'Ignore it,' said Davidson. 'Stick to the plan.'

Watkin pulled the lorry into the narrow street, entirely blocking it.

'Right, Watkin,' said Davidson, picking up his Stirling and getting out of the cab. 'Don't move from there until I get back.'

When he reached the back of the lorry, Sergeant Benbow and the rest of the men were climbing out. Davidson made a quick check of them. He saw that four remained inside. 'Good,' he said. 'Let's move Sergeant.'

They moved quickly round the corner and back into Micklegate. Sergeant Benbow stopped for a moment. 'I don't like it, sir,' he said. 'Something's up.'

But Davidson continued to make for the tall, Georgian terrace house. He flung open the door and went inside. He anticipated no real trouble. Sergeant Benbow saw the stairs leading down from the corridor on the right. 'Down here,' he said, standing aside for the four men to get past.

When Corporal Harrison reached the first floor, Davidson was already half-way up the next flight. 'Come on, lads,' he said, pushing through an open doorway on his right.

Davidson saw that there were attics above him. He sent two

men up, though he expected nothing up there. With his remaining two men, he searched the second floor rooms. There were four of them, and they were empty. In one of the rooms he found a desk and filing cabinets, with the drawers standing wide open. Only then did he begin to suspect that there had been a recent and hasty removal. He came out on to the central landing and called up to the attics. 'Anything up there?'

'Nothing, sir.'

'Better come down.'

The two men clattered down the stairs.

'Nothing at all?' said Davidson.

'Empty, sir. Nothing up there at all.'

Corporal Harrison on the floor below, had already come to the conclusion that there was no one in the building but themselves. A few empty boxes, an old overall and a pile of telephone directories, were the only things on the first floor. He knew he would have heard if anything had been found on the floors above or below him. 'All right, lads,' he said, gathering his four men together on the landing, 'check your weapons. And don't point the bloody things at me.'

Davidson clattered down the stairs ahead of his men. 'Well?' he said, when he saw Harrison.

'They've gone, sir,' said Harrison.

'Nothing?'

'Well, few boxes that's all. Nobody hiding in 'em—we've looked.'

'All right,' said Davidson. 'Come on.'

Davidson had visualized the scene for most of the night. He'd seen the members of the Central Committee together in one room, perhaps poring over maps, certainly engrossed in some planning operation. They were amazed to find themselves staring down the barrels of four or five Stirlings. They got up slowly, offering no resistance of any kind. Without speaking, they moved to the door and out into the street. The men in the lorry covered them whilst they climbed up the tailboard. Watkin had the engine started already. When Davidson slammed the passenger's door, they moved off at once. The whole operation had taken less than two minutes.

The reality was quite different. He wondered if they had

come to the wrong building. He wondered if the information given him in London had been wrong. He wondered . . .

'Sir?' Sergeant Benbow was calling from below.

'Coming, Sergeant,' called Davidson, going down to the ground floor.

'Place is empty,' said Benbow. 'Not a thing on this floor. Somebody's been here all right, but they've moved out in a hurry.'

'What about down there?' said Davidson, pointing down a further flight of stairs.

'Cellars, sir. Looks as if it's been some sort of club at one time. Few empty bottles. An old fruit machine. Hasn't been occupied for months.'

'Well,' said Davidson. He had no idea what to do.

'Wonder if we'd better move out, sir,' said Benbow. 'Out of town we can get the aerial up and contact HQ.'

'Don't teach him his job, Sarge,' muttered Harrison. 'He's got to learn sometime.'

'Mark my words, Harrison,' growled Benbow, without turning to face him, 'I'll have those bloody stripes off you if it's the last thing I do.'

'Right Sergeant,' said Davidson at last. 'Move the men out. I'll get the lorry started.' He ran down the street and round the corner into the lane.

'Some bloody officer,' said Corporal Harrison.

'Right you chaps!' cried Benbow.

Outside, Benbow caught sight of people standing behind open windows on the first floor of the houses opposite. The back of the furniture van had been dropped, but it was too dark to see what was inside. Standing in the doorway of the Adelphi Hotel was a man with a monocle. He was smiling. All Benbow's training and experience fused in a moment. He saw the situation with absolute clarity. It was not a question of having to make a decision. There was only one thing to do, as he saw it. 'Run for it lads,' he called. 'Quick as you can. Straight into the lorry.' He counted the men automatically as they rushed down the street and round the corner. By the time he began to follow them, Harrison was already on the corner shouting, 'Lorry's gone Sarge!'

'Straight down the lane, lads,' shouted Benbow. 'Run like hell.'

But half way down the lane Davidson was trying to pull away a barricade of straw bales, stretching from one wall to the other. Behind it stood men with rifles and shotguns. They were trapped. On one side were the brick walls of terrace houses. On the other, the five foot wall of St. Martin's churchyard, topped by three feet of iron railings.

'Let 'em have it!' cried Harrison, and sent a burst of automatic fire past Davidson, at the men behind the barricade.

Benbow saw the scene down the lane in front of him. 'Get into the doorways, lads!' he shouted. As he turned to face the guns in the houses opposite, he saw the furniture van begin to back up the street, turning to block off the only remaining escape from the lane. He gave a short burst with his Stirling at the tyres, but failed to stop its progress. Before he could fire again, Fitzwallace had hit him in the chest with a bullet from the rifle that had been propped out of sight in the doorway. Benbow turned and fell, as the van completed its manoeuvre and backed into the lane entrance. The troops were completely contained between the high walls, the barricade and the van. Men inside the van, again protected by straw bales, opened fire on them. Fire from the barricade cut them down. A few managed to get far enough into doorways to be safe for a minute or two. Then guns appeared over the churchyard wall, and the doorways were no longer any protection.

It lasted no more than two minutes. Then there was silence for some time. No one moved. The bodies in khaki lay slumped and sagged where they had fallen. The silence was almost deafening, after the reverberating clatter of automatic fire a few moments before. At last, the gaunt figure of Stephen Jackman, white-faced and shocked, rose from behind the straw bales blocking the lane. 'My God!' he said. 'What have we done?'

Davidson, slumped across the bales, groaned and turned over on his back. Jackman grabbed him by the shoulders of his khaki blouse, to prevent him slipping down on to the cobbles. 'He's still alive,' said Jackman, looking round for someone to help him. 'We must get him to hospital.'

Fitzwallace squeezed his way past the furniture van and into the lane. He was jubilant. 'Damn' good show,' he said. He had a ·38 Smith and Wesson in his hand. 'All right. No prisoners now. Lug the carcasses into the van.'

'This man's wounded,' cried Jackman.

'I should hope so,' said Fitzwallace.

'We must get him to hospital.'

'Don't be a damn' fool, man. Shoot him. Get him out of the way.'

'He must go to hospital,' insisted Jackman, still supporting Davidson over the bales.

Fitzwallace came up to him. 'Do you know what you're talking about?' he snapped, the monocle glinting from his eye in the sunlight. 'We're at war. War! Can't you get it into your head. If we show any quarter now we've lost. Shoot him. We've got to make an example of these people. How else can we show them we're in earnest?'

'He must go to hospital,' repeated Jackman, stubbornly.

Fitzwallace sensed that if he shot Davidson himself, he might not get away with it. He could feel the initial jubilation of success, was giving way to a deep sense of shock. Others at the barricade looked shocked by the noise and the bloodshed. At the moment he knew he could carry them with him, but perhaps not if he went any further. In any case, it was Jackman who must do the shooting, if any good was to come of it. Jackman must feel himself involved to the hilt. No, he thought, it can wait. The time will come. He caught sight of the insignia on Davidson's epaulettes. It was a way out. 'Quite right, Jackman,' he said with a quick smile. 'I didn't see he was an officer. He might be useful for interrogation purposes. See that he goes with the other one—the lorry driver. Get some medical attention for him. I'll talk to him later.'

Fitzwallace could feel the tension melt away as he turned from Jackman and the unconscious Davidson. Men came from behind the barricade, others dropped into the lane from the churchyard wall, and began to move the bodies into the furniture van. He had made the right decision. But he had seen something in Jackman during the confrontation—a stubborn quality of defiance, a tenacity over a principle—that he knew

61

must be removed. In a revolution, more than in a formal war, there must be absolute obedience to commands. At some convenient time in the future, Jackman would have to go.

4

THERE followed a period of unsureness on both sides, characteristic of such revolutions. The Council of the North was committed to militant action, by the St. Martin's Lane massacre. There was no withdrawal, short of total capitulation. On the other hand, no central government could compromise on the challenge that the Council had thrown down. There were many at that time on both sides, who would willingly have withdrawn from the positions they were in, but no dignified withdrawal was possible. The PM's position was made more complicated by the fact that no real news had reached London, concerning the fate of Ensign Davidson and his party. Davidson and Watkin, the driver of the lorry, were in the old condemned cell of the Debtor's Prison in York which formed part of the Castle Museum, but there was no way in which they could get a message out. They were, in any case, too unsure about their own fate to wish to jeopardize their position further by trying.

Although the five members of the Central Committee undoubtedly commanded the respect and loyalty of the North at that time—although for very different reasons—their very representativeness posed administrative difficulties. Most consultations with Rubinstein in Manchester and Brunton in Leeds, had to be conducted by telephone. Meetings of the entire Comittee could be held once or twice a week at the most. Wordsworth found himself making more and more of the day to day decisions. This suited his temperament, but it did mean that Fitzwallace felt free to take a more independent line too. It was also in his nature to act and then to account for his actions afterwards. Increasingly, Olsen was falling into his camp, as developments became more militant.

The lack of tight unity at the top, meant that supporters'

groups throughout the North were more difficult to control. There was no way of imposing real central authority. Again, since the general feeling was one of approaching liberation, there was an equally general reluctance to agree to a new discipline. There was a unity of the North, but an even stronger unity of towns and even districts of towns. The commander of a battalion of the King's Own Yorkshire Light Infantry, stationed in Pontefract, took it entirely on himself to occupy the BBC Regional Headquarters in Woodhouse Lane, Leeds, only to find to his utter disgust that all transmissions made from there could only actually be broadcast from Manchester. Quite independently, a senior officer at Catterick Camp, a fanatical supporter of Fitzwallace, shot dead the camp commandant because he refused to declare himself wholeheartedly behind the insurrection. When news of this reached the commander of the 2nd Battalion, The Lancashire Regiment, stationed near Poulton le Fylde, he marched on the RAF station outside Preston and persuaded the Commanding Officer there to declare himself for the North. At that time there were thirty-six operational Centaur low-level fighter bombers on the station.

All these developments brought their own additional complications. Southerners in Northern regiments began to desert and made their way south. Equally, Northerners in Southern regiments began to appear at Northern headquarters in increasing numbers. They came in most cases with their arms and equipment. Four pilots of the City of Leeds squadron, stationed at that time in Kent, flew their aircraft to Elvington in Yorkshire, an airfield that had not been in regular use for twenty years, to the general terror of local farmers and stock and the confusion of the Northern Air Force Command.

The position was similar in the South. A train from the North was boarded at Hitchin by troops of the Middlesex Regiment and all Northerners were forced to get off. The Australian touring team were advised not to play their games at Old Trafford and Headingley. The offices of the *Guardian* in Gray's Inn Road were sacked by students from the University of London, and most of the staff returned to Manchester.

It was the perennial problem of communications and control. Both commands at that time would have welcomed a pause.

They wanted to freeze all action and assess the situation coolly and objectively. But they calculated without the mood of the situation. The wave of Northern revolution could not be held. It caught up everyone in it. Insignificant personal actions escalated overnight into momentous developments. By the time news of them reached area commanders and the Central Committee, that news was hopelessly out of date. All orders issued by the higher commands were irrelevant to those on the spot, for they were issued on the assumption that a situation remained static at least long enough for top-level decisions to be taken on it.

The problem of the PM and his advisers was two-fold. In the first place, the lack of accurate information about precisely what was happening, made it impossible to see the situation whole. Rumours were inextricable from facts. Conjecture and eye-witness accounts could not be distinguished. Telephone communication between the South and many areas of the North had broken down. Radio communication was being constantly interfered with. Parliament clamoured for information but could never be satisfied. MPs themselves were torn in their allegiances. Many Northern MPs were convinced that if the conflict grew, they would have to withdraw from the House altogether since their first and overriding allegiance was to their constituents in the North. Almost twenty had already returned to the North. The most difficult position was that of the large number of Southerners who represented Northern constituencies in Parliament.

The second, and greater, problem facing the PM was the nature of the action he should take. His political experience told him that he must take the most stringent action at once. Troops must be sent in large numbers to crush the Northern rising. On the other hand, he was a Northerner himself. He sensed very clearly the nature of Northern aspirations. His father still lived in Liverpool. He had a sister in Carlisle and a brother in Thornaby. Worse than that, to send troops on a large scale against the North, was to set Englishmen at the throats of Englishmen. It had not been done in three hundred years. It would lead to the most bloody and bitter of all wars. Faced with this unenviable predicament, he continued for the next week simply to send small reconnaissance parties into the North with a view to clarifying his picture of the situation.

The Press had been clamouring for information from Wordsworth for days. Journalists stood day and night outside his house. There was always a group of ten or twelve outside the Committee headquarters in York. Whenever a member of the Committee moved, he was followed by journalists and photographers in cars and taxis. Wordsworth eventually called a press conference for the morning of June 3rd, in a conference room at the Royal Station Hotel.

Bill Gregson, a local free-lance, was at the meeting. He said afterwards: 'We had a hell of a job getting in. Press cards weren't much help. Everybody had to identify himself and his paper and be ticked off on a long list. Then we were searched— for weapons, I suppose. Nobody representing Southern papers got in—that meant nobody from the nationals. I got in by saying I was with the Evening Press boys. They were decent enough to back me up. All the foreign press agencies were there. I remember a blonde representing a dozen American provincial papers. She had just one question and she asked everybody it: "Is it your intention to call for American support?" I think it was the first thing she'd covered outside fashion. The Germans were there and the French and a couple of dark little men from Italy. I realized it was a lot bigger than anybody thought.

'Wordsworth made a statement to start the ball rolling. I got the impression of a very powerful man—big build, you know; ruthless maybe if you crossed him. Obviously very much in charge. He rolled his voice round the room and everybody listened. A bit like de Gaulle, but much heavier; he didn't smile and he wouldn't answer half the questions. I doubt if he'd run a press conference before—not on that scale. But he must have thought out every detail beforehand and probably rehearsed them too. He didn't put a foot wrong.

'None of the facts that Wordsworth handed out were much use to us. His statements were about general principles and the answers he gave to questions you could have taken in half a dozen ways. All very professional. But what did come over— and all Wordsworth's political manoeuvring couldn't hide it— was the tension between the five members of the Committee. No wonder. I've never seen five more different men apparently sold on the same policy. I say "apparently" because of course they were by no means all sold on it. Sir Felix Brunton was out of his depth. I doubt if he was even listening. He looked tired and drawn. His eyes looked as if they'd both been punched. He looked like an overworked concert pianist waiting for a badly conducted orchestra to get to his cue. He was there because of his name and his reputation as a liberal and a musician. He said nothing at all, and no one addressed a single remark to him.

'Rubinstein was different. Nobody would ever expect him to be out of his depth. But he was certainly out of sympathy. He said so, and Wordsworth couldn't stop him. "My views are well enough known," he said, in that fine fruity voice of his. "There is a pressing need for a Northern identity. Much of my life's work has been devoted to its creation. But I do not believe that any separate and permanent identity can be created by barbaric acts of force. The massacre in St. Martin's Lane was not the act of civilized men. If we do not preserve our humanity, then what is the meaning of freedom? I dissociate myself entirely from such barbarism. There will be no more of it whilst I remain on this Committee." He addressed his remarks more to Colonel Fitzwallace than to us. Fitzwallace was leaning back in his chair polishing his monocle. You would have thought to look at him that he saw nothing personal in Rubinstein's remarks. But you could feel the tension between the two men. A real subterranean struggle for power. A fundamental clash of philosophies. Wordsworth did what he could to turn aside the full force of Rubinstein's opposition. "You can see", he said, "how broad-based the views of the Committee are. Even at a time like this, we've not lost sight of—certain liberal principles." But I got the impression that Rubinstein would stay on the Committee only so long as he had control of GRANADA TV, and was prepared to use that control in support of a much more militant line of action.

'Fitzwallace was the real enigma. To begin with, most of us had hardly heard of him before. In their various ways, the others had all got national, if not international, reputations. But Fitzwallace was just a retired army officer with a fairly unspectacular career behind him. But he impressed us more than anyone else. Personally, if you'd asked me then, I'd have said that here was the real leader. It had something to do with his dramatic quality—a touch of showmanship I suppose. But it had far more to do with his sense of assuredness and ruthlessness. I got the impression that he knew exactly where he was going and that he wouldn't hesitate to use any means to get there. To judge from the easy charm, the authority in his voice, and particularly the plausible way in which he justified the St. Martin's Lane business, you couldn't help feeling that things were already going very much his way. Stockdale of the "Post" summed up the feelings of most of us when he said: "I like him. He's such a bloody villain."

'Olsen impressed the girl reporters, particularly the American blonde, with his good looks and his vitality. His reply to her question "Do you hope to get help from the States?" brought him a good deal of sympathy. "Well," he said, with that open smile of his, "in my business we've got accustomed to think of the States as looking to us for help." Frankly he didn't impress me. He was there because of his tremendous appeal to youth through the entertainers he controlled, and it showed. He talked at some length from a prepared script, about popular movements in the North. On specific issues he followed Fitzwallace's line to the letter. I wondered if Fitzwallace had written his script for him.

'Propped around the bar of the *Punchbowl* afterwards, we all agreed that as a press conference it had been a hell of a waste of time. Nobody had answered any important questions. Nobody had given us any of those hard dramatic facts on which you build news. And yet a lot had come across. There was this obvious disunity at the top about basic aims. There was a clear struggle for power in the Central Committee, principally as I saw it between Wordsworth and Fitzwallace, though Rubinstein could hardly be ignored. Somebody, it was obvious, was going to make a big move soon in order to secure absolute authority. My shirt was really on Wordsworth, simply because of his money and his connections. Not only could he do it, but he had the will to do it. Fitzwallace, I confess, I rather thought of as a bit of a swashbuckler—a soldier of fortune. Anyway, that's the impression I got. How wrong can you be?'

Valerie Paine got back to the flat in Cadogan Square a little after 8 p.m. on June 3rd. She had spent ten days in Nice with the son of a General Motors executive, eight years her junior. She was in a furious temper, having been held up at London Airport for two hours by a strike of ground staff. Paine was working at his desk in the window of the lounge. Papers were piled carefully on the floor around him. He began to get up as she came into the room.

'Oh, for God's sake sit down,' she said, tossing her handbag on the table and dropping into an armchair.

'I'll make you some tea,' he said, picking up his stick.

'Don't be a martyr. If I want it, I can get it myself.'

'The trip, I gather, wasn't very successful. I'd be glad if you'd take it out on someone else. I'm rather tired.' He continued to walk across the room and out into the kitchen.

'You're right,' she called after him. 'A complete fiasco . . . I'm sorry.'

She continued to lie in the armchair. She could hear him filling the kettle and opening the china cupboard. She picked up a copy of *She* from the little table at her side and turned the pages over without really looking at them. She got up and looked out of the window at the square. There were pigeons on the pavement opposite, picking between the cracks of the stones. She looked at herself in the mirror, licked her finger and rubbed a smut off her nose. When Paine looked round for the teapot, she was standing in the doorway watching him. She smiled and he smiled back.

'Robert, you're very understanding. I'm sorry. I've given you a pretty miserable life I suppose. Well I don't *suppose*— I know. But who am I? Can you tell me that? Look at you— you've got all this work to absorb you. You're mind's occupied with momentous things. What have I got—no, really? What can I think about, day in day out, but me? Most of the time I think I'm not really worth thinking about. I get so bored! I'm caught somehow—trapped. I must get out. You don't know the feeling, do you? And when I get out . . .'

'That's how it was, was it?'

She dropped her hands from the door frame and got the milk out of the fridge. 'It always is. Fine for the first few hours —new, thrilling, exciting. New places, new faces, new sensations. Then it palls. Then I wonder. Finally I feel sick. Why do I run back home? Do you know?'

'No,' he said.

'You don't mind me coming back? You don't think it would be better if I just stayed away for good?'

'You're my wife.'

'Is that all you think? Is that all that's left to us—man and wife?'

'I should have thought that was quite a lot. Something solid—permanent.'

'Good God!' she said. 'Solid. Permanent. Like a millstone. Like the Rock of Gibraltar. You haven't made love to me in six months. We haven't been out together since Christmas. Not once. What kind of a solid, permanent relationship is that? Look . . . let's just drop everything now. Let's leave the tea and go out. Now—this very second. We can have a meal in Caporelli's. I'm starving, you know.'

'I'm sorry,' he said, pouring out the tea. 'I've a stack of work.'

'I see,' she said.

'You go out.'

'No,' she said, picking up the two cups of tea and taking them into the lounge. 'No, I'll stay at home. I'll be as dutiful as hell. I'll stay around to warm your slippers if it suddenly gets frosty. There'll be a tin of something in the kitchen. I can make do on that.'

'There's chicken in the fridge.'

'Well then, I can eat the chicken from the fridge can't I? Then when you've finished your work, we can sit and chat can't we? God, why didn't they teach me to knit at school?' She sat down. 'Perhaps if I took up religion, do you think?

70

Does one take up religion, or do you just sit around and wait to catch it? And how, by the way, is the war going?'

'The war?'

'I know. There are so many. Our war. The one the continental papers are full of. You know—the bears up in the North.'

'I've seen the papers. They exaggerate.'

'Do they now. This York massacre, the occupation of the BBC station in Leeds, the sacking of the *Guardian* office in London . . .'

'They're still only isolated incidents.'

'Really?'

'I admit they're serious.'

'Well that's an admission! I wonder if anyone down here knows what these people are like.'

'Do you?'

'I knew Colonel Fitzwallace. *Paris Match* has a cover picture of him.'

'Knew him—intimately, I suppose?' said Paine, limping to his desk.

'How else can one say one knows a man?'

'I met him in York. He told me. He sent you his most fond remembrances. It was all a little painful.'

'I'm sorry.'

'But your Colonel Fitzwallace is a murderer and a traitor. When he's caught he'll no doubt be hanged.'

'I suppose so. But you've not caught him yet?'

'We shall.' He sat down at the desk and took up his pen. The sight of his back, arched over his papers, infuriated her. At times she felt she was losing her hold over him. She got up and walked over to him and put her hands gently on his shoulders.

'I'm rather busy . . . ' he said.

'You know,' she said lightly, 'I could catch him for you. He'd see me.'

'No doubt.'

'There can't be many others who could get to him.'

'There are some, I believe.'

'But you'll bear the offer in mind, Robert, won't you?'

'Yes,' he said. 'I'll bear it in mind.'

It was characteristic of Valerie Paine that having sown the seed she should begin to nurture it. She took a sheet of official paper from a pigeon-hole in the desk and sat down at the table to write a letter.

Blackett was standing with his back to the window. He spoke, not so much with fire as with a deep and savage tenacity. He had that single-mindedness, that sense of power unified and clearly directed, that appears in the more militant pictures of Churchill during the Second World War. He said to Fitzwallace: 'It's too late for compromise. The choice has been made. It's got to be followed through.'

'Some limited military action against the South,' said Fitzwallace. 'How would you see that?'

'When?'

'That would depend.'

'Logical. An inevitable next step. Some concrete backing's necessary for the *Declaration of Separateness*. Perhaps reprisals for the St. Martin's Lane attack.'

'Where would the Council for the North stand?'

'With you,' said Blackett. 'Naturally.'

'And Rubinstein?'

'Don't you know?'

'I know—do you?'

'He'd be tooth and nail against it. These liberals . . .'

'Which would leave one of our most powerful communications systems in neutral hands,' said Fitzwallace, more to himself than to Blackett. 'The others have given us their backing.'

'At best, neutral,' said Blackett. But it was clear from his manner that he was considering such a development at its worst.

Fitzwallace rang Bainbridge, who had taken over control of Catterick Camp, to make sure of his support, and then took the evening train to Manchester. He had a meeting planned with

Brigadier John Macey, whose brilliance in guerilla tactics in Colombia and Borneo had already assured him a place in military history, and who had risen in the last few weeks to be the most militant voice in the North-west.

It was a damp and oppressive evening. Fitzwallace opened the window of the compartment, and all the smells of industrial Yorkshire blew in. Only a storm could clear the air and make it fit to breathe again. To the north of Leeds, there were already a few flashes of lightning. At every station there were troops, and at level crossings and by the side of trunk roads in the open country, groups of civilians were building sandbag emplacements. Many of them carried rifles. All wore armbands bearing the single letter N.

In Huddersfield, Fitzwallace had a seven minute meeting on the train with Sigsworth, the local commander. There was no question about it, feeling was running very high. There was enthusiasm and activity everywhere. One thing was clear to Fitzwallace above everything else; in its present fever, the North would stand for nothing short of Southern capitulation. Even Sigsworth, responsible only for the comparatively small and thinly populated area from Huddersfield to the Lancashire border, was anxious to know when he could begin to move south.

Macey was on Exchange Station when Fitzwallace's train pulled in. He looked ridiculous in a sagging bush hat and an entirely ludicrous uniform made of a dozen different pieces from army surplus stores. He was fat and red-faced and smoked a cigar. The energy seemed to burst out of him. 'My dear chap,' he growled, gripping Fitzwallace by the hand. His breath smelt of whiskey. He looked and behaved like a Hollywood Mexican bandit.

'John,' said Fitzwallace, adjusting his monocle.

There were at least twenty men round Macey, dressed as eccentrically as their leader. They cleared a way through the other passengers to the waiting room, which Macey had arranged for the conference. There was a long table down the middle, made of planks on trestles, and round it a dozen chairs. On the table itself were pads of paper, pencils, two bottles of Scotch, glasses and a bottle of water. Macey threw his hat on the table and poured out two drinks. 'Well Douglas' he said, screwing his broad backside on to the edge of the table. 'Do we march?'

Fitzwallace sat down and polished his monocle. He looked round the bare room and at the men standing on guard inside the door. 'With these men?' he asked, distastefully.

'Yes,' cried Macey, finishing his drink and banging the glass down on the table. 'With these men!'

'I don't think you appreciate the position,' said Fitzwallace quickly. 'We are at war—war. War demands discipline. Obedience. I came here under the impression that you had under your command an army. What do I find? These—' he waved a disparaging hand towards the men by the door '—bandits.'

'Bandits!' cried Macey, lifting himself off the table. 'Let me tell you that bandits like these did very well in the mountains of Colombia.'

'And let me tell you that we are not fighting untrained riff-raff in the mountains of Colombia or the jungles of Borneo. I know your record. Do you think I'd put up with you for a moment if I didn't? But here the situation is different. In the field against us will be highly trained troops—the best in Europe—equipped with mortars and field-pieces, tanks, automatic weapons and aircraft—everything that military ingenuity can provide. They'll be fighting on their home ground. They'll be defending their own possessions. They won't be mercenaries fighting for somebody else's political convictions, they'll be men fighting for their own homes and families.'

'Well all right,' growled Macey.

'Against that kind of opposition we need a hand-picked army, perfectly motivated, intelligent, highly trained, perfectly disciplined, brilliantly and imaginatively led. I've no doubt you have the men—the raw material, the grist. I know such a leader exists, because I know your reputation is legendary. But the discipline, the hard polish, the diamond finish—I see no sign of it. Do I make myself quite clear?'

'Yes,' snapped Macey. He poured himself another drink and when he had drunk it, he set the glass down carefully on the table. Finally his innate good humour broke through. He began

74

to smile and then to laugh. 'Yes,' he cried, 'you make yourself quite clear.' He picked up his hat from the table and crammed it into the hands of a man at his side. 'Get rid of this,' he said. 'And issue uniforms and armbands from the Ancoats store. And the rest of you—wait outside.' He sat down and waited until the door had closed behind them. Then he said: 'Pity you had to take me to task in front of my men.'

'What choice did you leave me?' said Fitzwallace.

'None—of course!' laughed Macey.

Fitzwallace took two maps from his briefcase and spread them on the table. One was of the central area of Manchester, the other was of England and Wales from the Humber to the south coast. 'Now the operation will be in two distinct parts.' He drew the Manchester map towards him and dropped the point of his pencil on a building that had already been ringed in red. 'Part one will be the occupation of this building and the removal of a man called Rubinstein . . . '

The Diary of Brigadier John Macey published recently in America, contains this entry for June 3rd:

'Fitzwallace: a born leader—ambitious, cool, single-minded. Had doubts about him at first—too much the actor perhaps? His reputation with women not very encouraging either. But he came into the meeting to-day bent on establishing his authority. I've no doubts any longer. The breadth of his strategic vision and the precisely conceived specific aims were enough for me. Fitzwallace is for the North, and I'm for Fitzwallace. Our immediate objective is the occupation of the GRANADA TV building off Deansgate and the removal of the top man. Fitzwallace anticipates no opposition. He already has a team working in the building, capable of taking over the broadcasting of news and general information. I shall need 50 men with light automatic weapons. If we can occupy the principal control points within the first ten minutes, then the show will be over.'

The letter that Valerie Paine had written to the PM's Personal Private Secretary, inevitably reached the PM. The PPS thought at first of destroying it, since it was going to be such an embarrassment to Paine himself. But that would only shelve the problem. She would write again. In any case, in her very special position as Paine's wife there were ways in which she could approach the PM direct. The PPS hoped that in any case the PM would simply toss it aside as being the suggestion of an amateur dabbler. Instead, after he had glanced through it he called Paine in.

'Know anything about this, Robert?' he said, passing him the letter.

Paine took the letter. He pointed to a chair. 'Do you mind if I sit for a moment, sir?'

The PM waved a hand towards him and he sat down. He recognised the writing at once. His heart sank. He had been in this position so many times; called on to explain another wild and embarrassing indiscretion, about which he knew nothing. 'I'm sorry,' he muttered automatically.

'What for? At least it's a suggestion. Question is whether she'd be any use to us. What do you think?'

'Well—I think what she says is probably true enough. I've no reason to disbelieve her when she says she knows Fitzwallace well . . .'

'Look, Robert, I'm giving instructions for general mobilization tonight. But I'm in the dark. I can't find out exactly what's going on up there. I must know before they make another major move. I was turned back, as you know. I sent up a party of troops—absolute silence. Rumours of course, but am I to act on rumours? They've got road blocks on all entries to the North. They stop and search every train that goes up. Every aircraft passenger is vetted before he's allowed to land. Never mind this nonsense about catching Fitzwallace. In any case, if we caught him now and made an example of him, we'd have the whole North marching on us. But can she do three things? Can she get through to Fitzwallace; can she find out something definite about his plans; can she get that information back to us here?'

He swivelled his chair round to face his desk and began to turn over a sheaf of papers. Paine leaned forward, his hands resting on the handle of his stick. He knew that if his wife

76

claimed to be able to get through to Fitzwallace, then the chances were that nothing would stand in her way. The excitement of the enterprise was the kind of thing she revelled in. Any challenge brought out all her ingenuity and resources. He would have to say 'yes' to the PM's questions, but at the back of his mind was the unpredictability of the woman.

'I think the answer to all three of your questions, must be "yes",' he said.

'But you've some reservation?'

'Prime Minister—I don't really know my wife. Certainly I don't understand her. In fairness to the country I must say I find her unpredictable—even unreliable. If you'd asked the question, *will* she get through and *will* she get the information back here . . .'

'But that wasn't the question I asked. It's sufficient for me if you think she *can*. And that's what you're saying, isn't it?'

Paine nodded. 'Yes, sir,' he said.

'Then that's a start. No point in picking someone reliable we know hasn't a chance in hell of getting through. If she can get through, we can question her reliability later. We might find after all that we're doing her an injustice to question it.' He took a sealed foolscap envelope from a tray and handed it to Paine. 'See that this reaches her as soon as possible, Robert. It contains all instructions, maps, authorization and the like. The official documents of identity will get her as far as Nottinghamshire. After that she'd better get rid of them. Impress upon her the urgency, will you? And Robert—I appreciate what this is costing you personally. I want you to know I'm grateful.'

Valerie Paine left King's Cross at 7.30 the same evening. She was dressed as inconspicuously as was possible for her, in a navy linen suit and a small hat of navy straw. But she was not the sort of person ever to pass unnoticed. The very simplicity of her outfit lent a certain drama and mystery to her face. Her fair hair was even more striking under the dark hat. And she had not been able to resist the temptation to wear a large ruby and diamond clasp in the lapel of her jacket. Men stared as she followed the porter along the platform. She felt them staring and she was glad. Inconspicuousness was one thing, insignificance quite another.

She travelled alone in a first-class compartment, rechecked the contents of the PM's envelope, read a little, and then went for dinner. Back in the compartment after dinner, she fell into a light sleep. It must have been about 9.30 when the train stopped with a long screech of brakes and woke her up. She could not for the moment remember where she was. There were shouts when the train finally came to a halt. Doors opened and she could hear feet clattering along the corridor. The blinds on the corridor side of her compartment were down, so it was not until two soldiers slid open the door and pointed sub-machine guns at her, that she began to realize what had happened.

'That your case?' said one of the men. He was in khaki battledress and beret, and wore an armband bearing the letter N in black. He had spots of an angry purple down one of his cheeks. Valerie judged him to be about twenty-one.

'Yes,' she said. 'And who are you?'

'Get it down will you Jack?' he said to his companion, who pushed into the compartment and pulled the case off the rack.

'What are you doing?' said Valerie, now fully awake.

'Everybody off,' said the soldier. 'That includes you.' He backed out of the doorway and beckoned her to follow him with a sharp gesture of his gun. She got up and turned automatically to look at herself in the mirror over the opposite seat. 'Out!' he cried.

On the platform, it was clear that everyone was getting off.

'Down there,' said the soldier, indicating the far end of the platform with a nod of his head.

'But please tell me what's happening,' she said, beginning to feel a genuine concern.

'Haven't you heard? There's a war on.'

She saw the word *Retford* on a bench. There was a queue at the end of the platform. When she got nearer she saw that wooden barriers had been erected to filter the crowd into a funnel. Across the end of the funnel was a trestle table at which sat an officer and two men. Soldiers stood about in groups beyond. At the table she was asked her name, address and destination. The officer laughed when she told him she had been summoned by Colonel Fitzwallace. She showed him one of the official documents she carried, hoping that the official seals and signatures would impress him. He tore it up without looking at it. 'Through there,' he said. 'On the left.'

She joined a group of totally perplexed people, carrying a clutter of bags and suitcases. Ten minutes went past, and then the officer got up from the table and came over to them. 'All right, you Southerners,' he cried. 'Gather round.' There were protests and demands from the group, but he ignored them all. 'The line's closed to the North. Make your way round to that platform. We're stopping the south bound for you.'

'What's happening?' said a man with a large briefcase. 'It's a scandal,' said a woman, trying to quieten a child in her arms. 'I demand . . .' cried the man with the briefcase. A soldier pushed him out of the way with his rifle.

In the confusion, Valerie got out of the station and found a taxi. 'Take me to York,' she said to the driver as she pushed her suitcase into the back.

'You're joking,' said the driver, without looking at her. He was picking his teeth with a matchstick.

'Well then, how far can you take me?' There seemed no point in arguing with him.

'Might get you to Bawtry. Have to go the side roads. Run up a fair old mileage.'

'I'll pay.'

'Course you'll pay, lady.'

Clear of the town, the taxi driver became more communicative. They were at war, he was clear about that. He wasn't sure what the position was in Nottinghamshire, but further north they'd broken with London. 'Serve 'em damn' well right,' he commented. Valerie couldn't make out which side he was referring to. What she did realize, was that during her journey some significant piece of news had broken.

5

FITZWALLACE stayed in Manchester to supervise the carrying out of the first stage of his plan. Macey, dressed in more orthodox uniform, was still sufficiently independent to insist on leading his men personally against GRANADA TV. Fitzwallace pointed out the consequences to the movement in the North-west if Macey was killed. His reply was characteristic: 'In that event I shall lose interest in the movement anyway.'

There was, of course, no opposition. In the first place, the move against the television station was completely unexpected, except by those people working there who had been instructed by Fitzwallace to take over its day to day working. In the second place, Manchester was such a citadel of Northern aspirations that had news of the plan leaked out, its citizens would most likely have supported rather than opposed Macey. It was inconceivable to anyone that the attack was in essence against Rubinstein himself, who had done so much to crystallize Northern sentiment. Almost alone, he and those in control before him had created the new North by consistently broadcasting their image of it.

Macey called the duty staff together and explained that in the interests of Northern security, the building and the transmitter had been occupied by the Council of the North. 'There are rumours,' he said, 'of a plot to put Southern troops here. You'll appreciate what damage that could do to the North. A transmitter as powerful as this in our very middle.' He pointed out that the traditional policy of providing Northern programmes and Northern news for the North, would continue unchanged. Passes, of course, would have to be issued during the emergency and he was sorry that it would be necessary for him to leave troops on the premises to prevent any attempt at sabotage. But he assured them that, but for these minor irritations, the majority would notice no difference whatever in the life of the building. He said that he appreciated that there might be a few members of the staff who would not wish to continue working there. These, he said, would be quite free to leave. If there were any who wished for safe conduct 'over the southern frontier', as he described it, that safe conduct would be given.

'Time's pressing, ladies and gentlemen,' he concluded, with a glance at the clock on the wall. 'I can give you five minutes to make up your minds whether you wish to stay on or whether you wish to resign.' He sat down on the table corner and swung a thick leg to and fro.

Five minutes, as Macey had intended, gave no one any chance to make the tremendous decision he had forced on them. Many hadn't fully understood what the appearance of Macey and his troops really signified. Those who were privy to Fitzwallace's plan beforehand, spent the time convincing the remainder that the work of the company would go on as before. In any case, most of the staff were Northerners by birth or adoption. They were behind any move that appeared to be in the general Northern interest. In the end, only two men elected to leave. They had come up together from the BBC Television Centre in Shepherd's Bush, only two weeks earlier. True to his word, Macey had them escorted to the station and given safe conduct on the next train south.

From 5.15 p.m. a message was broadcast on all Northern TV networks, at fifteen minute intervals. It ran: 'We should like to remind you that at 7.30 this evening Colonel Fitzwallace of the Central Committee will be making a most important announcement. That's at half-past seven, immediately before *Coronation Street*. Programmes for the rest of the evening will run approximately ten minutes late.' Northern press staffs stood by to issue special editions immediately after the announcement.

An hour later—a little after 6 p.m.—Fitzwallace reached the building. 'Admirable, John,' he said, shaking Macey vigorously by the hand. 'No trouble?'

'Walked straight in,' said Macey. 'No opposition at all.

Talked to the staff and they're all back at work. I've got a producer or somebody, and some other chaps waiting for you upstairs. We've got lines through to TYNE-TEES and YORKSHIRE TV.'

'Admirable,' said Fitzwallace again. He seemed extremely pleased with the way things had gone. He carried a swordstick which he tapped on the tiles as he strode about the large entrance hall. 'And what about —?' He pointed upstairs with his stick.

'Still up there. I've two men with him. Thought I'd better not do anything till you saw him.'

'Quite right,' said Fitzwallace. 'Well: he can wait. Make sure he doesn't get near the controls. Shall we run up and see this producer fellow?'

Before his broadcast, Fitzwallace spoke to Olsen on the phone. 'A very tricky situation, Sidney,' he said. 'Have I your support for acting?'

'Of course,' said Olsen. 'Whatever you think best.'

'Get hold of Blackett. Tell him to watch the broadcast at 7.30.'

'I'll tell him. He's probably seen the announcements already. Everyone's talking about them; but I'll make sure he knows. What about Wordsworth?'

'I wouldn't bother,' said Fitzwallace.

Wordsworth in fact saw the announcement at 6.45 p.m. His phone call to GRANADA eventually reached Macey. 'Well,' said Macey, 'I'll see if he's about.'

'Damn the man,' said Fitzwallace. 'Let him wait five minutes then tell him I can't be found.' He put through a call to Sir Felix Brunton but he was rehearsing in Halifax. 'These music makers,' he said. 'Never can get hold of them in a crisis.' But he seemed not in the least perturbed. At 7.30 p.m., he appeared before the cameras.

He was an impressive figure on television, with his clear-cut features, his sparkling monocle and his easy, immediate charm. He gave the impression to the ordinary viewer, not of a leader speaking from some inner, oak-panelled sanctum, but of a tremendous personal friend. He managed to convey by his assurance, the impression that he was the real power in the

North, in such a way that his authority was never questioned. He knew too precisely the nature of the viewer to whom he was speaking. Not the intellectual, although he was not excluded, but the men and women on whom was falling the burden of keeping the means of production going, and to those whose support he was already calling upon for active service in the field.

'. . . and so,' he concluded, 'on behalf of the Council of the North, whose servant—after all—I am, I'm here to tell you that at half-past seven this evening the counties of Cumberland, Westmorland, Lancashire, Northumberland, Durham and Yorkshire, became an independent state with its capital in the ancient city of York. From that moment we were free of the tyrannies of London and the South-east. Free to make our own laws. Free to spend our own money on our own needs. Free for the first time in a thousand years—ever since those French came over and stole our land and belongings.' He poured out a glass of water from the carafe on the table, and lifted it to the television camera. 'Friends,' he said, with burning sincerity, 'Northerners, fellow countrymen. I give you The North.'

'A damn' fine performance,' said Macey, who had been watching on a monitor in the control room. 'You're a born actor. Real sincerity. You've hooked the lot of 'em.'

'You're mistaken John,' said Fitzwallace crisply. 'On this point at least, I *am* sincere.'

'Well—sincere or not, what's it matter. There's not a man or woman who wouldn't march with you now.'

'I hope you're right, for there's marching to be done.'

'Well!' said Macey, getting off the table edge, and tapping the back of a chair with his cane.

'Are the men ready?'

'We can move at nine.'

'Good.' He put out his hand to Macey. 'See you in twenty-four hours.'

'You should be coming with us,' said Macey with a sudden roar of laughter. 'Can't you just see us mixing it with all those long-haired puffs?'

'One thing John; don't mix it for too long. This is a raiding party, not a full-scale attack. We want to show them we mean business, that's all. We can't hope for conquest. Not yet, anyway. Whatever success you have, you're not to try to consolidate it. I want you in quickly and out again twice as quickly. You're quite clear?'

'Clear enough,' said Macey. 'Don't worry yourself. With the numbers I've got I'm not thinking of conquest.'

'Give the bastards stick,' said Fitzwallace. 'And—good luck!'

Macey and his men moved off in trucks and light armoured vehicles at 9 p.m., leaving Manchester by the Wilmslow Road. It was Macey's intention to keep, as far as possible, to secondary roads, at least until he was well into Southern territory. The problem was to know where exactly the frontier of sympathy between the two areas of the country lay. With his small force, he had to rely solely on surprise to reach his objective. He couldn't risk any large-scale confrontation. He planned to keep well clear of Derby and to join M1 at the Markfield access point during the hours of darkness. If all went well, he would be moving down Western Avenue at 4 the next morning. By 6 he expected to be pulling out for the North. All however, did not go well.

Stephen Jackman, sitting at home watching Fitzwallace's broadcast, muttered aloud to himself: 'That man is mad. There are ways of doing things and this isn't one of them.' Dr. Colin Blackett, however, watching on a portable TV set that he had brought into his consulting room especially for the broadcast, said to his receptionist: 'Thank God someone has the guts to make a move.' The broadcast in fact split the Council of the North down the middle. At the same time it completely isolated Wordsworth in the Central Committee.

But despite doubts amongst members of the Council, the broadcast had the effect of injecting a new burst of vitality into the vast majority of people who saw it. The sense of national unity and purpose was greatly intensified. In Halifax, the regional headquarters of the London Provincial Development Corporation were sacked because of the Corporation's name and because of a rumour running through the town that the two principal backers were retired City men with homes in Bognor Regis. The same Corporation's regional offices in Wigan and Middlesbrough were burnt to the ground. Perhaps strangely, the feeling was not one of general xenophobia, but was quite specifically directed against London in the rather wide Northern definition of that place. In Bradford, for example, the Pakistani and Polish populations were as active as the rest of the community in smashing the windows of all London-based banks in the city. In Leeds, it was coloured students from Ghana and the West Indies who burnt an effigy of 'the typical Londoner' on the steps of the Town Hall.

York had a certain reputation for its Festival of the Arts, which began that year on June 1st. Attempts by the Festival Committee to cancel the event in view of the impending hostilities, had been violently opposed by the new Festival Administrator. Czezny, the Administrator, was short, aggressive and bitterly determined. By birth he was a Pole. He had escaped to England in 1939 and fought during the war with the Free Polish Air Force. His eye was constantly on the international scene and he refused even to acknowledge the existence of local life. His declared aim was to establish in a small provincial city, a festival of international repute. The view of the Festival Committee was this: a festival of international repute cannot be supported solely by the residents of the area in which it takes place. The bulk of its support must come from outside. York, rapidly becoming the centre of what was in effect a civil war, could hardly continue to attract outsiders interested in the arts. It was unfortunate that the principal factor in Czezny's make-up that had driven him to his present position of very considerable influence, was a sense of isolation and persecution. His need to dominate was essentially a fight in him for security. Power, he seemed to feel, alone could balance isolation. Classically, of course, power itself isolates, so that the more he fought for it the more isolated he became. It was this personal temperamental bias that made him react to his Committee's very reasonable suggestion to cancel the Festival, as if it were a penetrating and concerted attack on him personally. He talked of the position that he could give York in the international field of the arts. He talked of the artists with international reputations who were already in the City rehearsing. He talked of the laughing stock that would be made of the Festival Committee itself throughout the cultural capitals of the world. He touched that sense of inadequacy and inferiority that most provincials and all Northerners feel, when faced by a man talking about art and culture on an international scale. The Committee, very much against the better judgement of its members, changed its mind.

The spectacle of an international festival being launched without international support and at the centre of a civil war, might on the face of it seem amusing. Perhaps to those Americans who read the article by James Roderik in *Life,* it was amusing. But there was a significant point that Roderik missed. International art is concerned with international, not local, aspirations. It imposes an international discipline and system of judgement, by comparison with which local creativity must appear inferior. The very internationalism of Czezny's intention had already produced an explosive situation. Many people had wondered what the point was of international art, when it was accompanied by an attitude of monumental disdain for local aspirations. And again—a further point that Roderik missed—international artists tend to live in capital cities. In England, London more than any other city is where English artists with an international reputation live. A glance at the Festival programme for that year, was enough to convince anyone with any sensitivity to the situation, that it could only lead to disaster. On the evening of June 3rd, *The London Mozart Strings* were playing Vivaldi in the Guildhall, *The London Opera Group* were giving a concert of excerpts from the works of Verdi, Mozart and Rossini in the Tempest Anderson Hall, *The Cambridge Footlights* were appearing at the Joseph Rowntree Theatre and the *London Madrigal Songsters* were performing in the hall of the Merchant Adventurers.

Bill Gregson was supposed to be covering the Vivaldi for the *Guardian.* He said later: 'Ken Adams had to cover it for the *Post.* We tossed for it and I won. Ken promised me a carbon of the story later that evening, so I went to the *Mystery Plays* instead. I'd never seen them. They're the centre of the whole thing really. But then, it was a warm, clear evening. I preferred to see something in the open, rather than getting shut up with Vivaldi in the Guildhall. I could hear shouting from the town outside. Perhaps it was singing more than shouting.

'Granville Bellamy was playing Christ. And he was good— no, brilliant. I couldn't take my eyes off him. I didn't really know what to expect, because there was a lot of feeling against him in the town. They'd billed him—the damn' fools—as "the great West End star". He was a West End actor, but did they have to shove it on all the posters at a time like that? There was this other story too, that he'd seduced the Virgin Mary. She was the daughter of some local county chap. Nobody liked that either. But then, if a girl plays around with amateur dramatics what does she expect? If it hadn't been Bellamy, it would have been somebody else.

'We got to the crucifixion spot. The lights threw him and those nearest him into high prominence. On the edges of the light there were the crowds of citizens of Jerusalem and the Roman soldiers pushing them out of the way. It was a blinding performance by Bellamy. He really was terrific. I'm not much moved by the theatre, but this—! I began to sweat in the palms of my hands as he dragged forward, step by painful step, with that great crude weight of wood across his shoulder. I tell you, if I'd been nearer I'd have helped him—just got up there and then and taken some of the weight off his sagging body. The sweat on his forehead glistened under the lights. A woman in a long blue dress put up a cloth to mop his face. I wanted to shout out when a Roman soldier pushed her aside and she dropped sobbing to her knees. It wasn't hushed, you know. Not like being in church. It was noisy, with the crowd pushing forward and shouting. Some jeered. Some looked drunk and festive. And the noise wasn't confined to the stage: it spread out over the Museum Gardens and into the body of the town behind me. And the crowd seemed to increase. It didn't seem any longer confined to the stage. It looked to be spreading out beyond the stage and up into the audience. I felt myself becoming part of it. It sucked me into itself. I felt a shout coming up in my throat. Everyone seemed to be shouting. Then it began to dawn on me —you know what it's like as a journalist: part of you always steers clear of total involvement—the bulk of the crowd wasn't actors at all. They were real people; people from the town who'd swarmed into the place. It was an invasion from outside. When it finally clicked with me, Bellamy was about half-way across the lower level. I don't think he noticed them even then. There must have been a hundred of them and there were far more crushing in behind them. "We want Jesus! We want Jesus!" they were chanting. I tell you, I was terrified. The volume of sound got louder as more of them took up the chant. Bellamy saw them when they began to climb on to the stage. He clearly didn't know what was going on. He had this great wooden cross still over one shoulder. They went right up to him and stood all the way round him. From where I was, I could see over their heads. One of them stepped forward with a rope. I thought to God for one crucifying moment they were going to hang him. I found myself standing up shouting "No! No!" but nobody heard me above the din.

'Some of the school kids had begun to cry. I doubt if many of them could see what was going on from where they were sitting, but the atmosphere would have put the fear of God up anyone. A number of soldiers wearing armbands and carrying rifles or light automatic weapons, stood about near the stage.

'Then they moved in on him with the rope. Three or four took the weight of the cross. He must have fallen, for he disappeared from sight. Somebody shouted: "Crucify the Southern bastard!" and struck downwards with a rifle butt. I stood absolutely frozen where I was. The stage was in hopeless confusion, with the actors running out of sight round the abbey wall and the rest crowding this way and that, chanting all the time. There was a good deal of laughter and some jeering. Finally something was being lifted above the heads of the crowd, right into the light of a spot. I knew it was Bellamy by the colour of his costume, although it had been torn off his shoulders. They had roped his arms and legs to the cross. They carried him a yard or two to the left and got the base of the cross in the hole. There was some pushing and shouting before they finally got it erected. Then as they moved away from it, I could see Bellamy roped securely to it, his head lolling drunkenly to one side.

'The crowd seemed more high-spirited than violent. If it

hadn't been for Bellamy, hanging there in that spotlight, I would have thought it was a cup-final crowd on the spree. Suddenly a figure appeared on the high-level scaffolding, half-way up the wall of the abbey. Someone got a spotlight on it. It was a man in dinner jacket and bowtie shouting through a loudhailer. I could tell from the stance—pugnacious, you know; crouched low with feet apart—that it was Czezny. "Stop, stop, stop!" he was screaming. The crowd began to notice him. It quietened. A few people shouted at him. "You scum!" he screamed. "You filthy—filthy scum! Swine! Swine!" His voice boomed through that electrical contraption till I thought I'd go mad. It hit the walls of the abbey and boomed back again. He was beside himself with rage. The words he wanted to express his feelings wouldn't come. I doubt if such words exist. "You have destroyed a work of art! You have destroyed the work of God himself! You have desecrated holy ground! Murderers!" I remember the word shook my very fibres. I didn't think Bellamy was dead. He didn't look dead. But then Czezny was nearer than I was. Some beast is abroad, I remember thinking. Nobody can call it by its name and nobody can control it. I felt the beginning of the end of the world—believe me. Somebody began to laugh and mimic Czezny's accent. The crowd laughed uncontrollably. Czezny picked up a property spear and hurled it at the crowd. I thought, what he wouldn't give for a machine gun to demolish us all. There was a scream. The spear had struck a girl in the chest. The laughter stopped. The crowd bubbled like porridge. "He's killed her!" somebody cried in amazement. "You filthy Northern swine!" Czezny screamed, the loudhailer right up to his lips. "Kill him," somebody shouted. "She's dead. Kill him!" shouted a woman. As the crowd rushed for the ladder leading to the high scaffold, I saw a soldier down on my left lift his automatic. There was nothing that could have saved Czezny then. The burst of firing seemed to go on endlessly. I saw the bullets strike the stonework on one side of Czezny, cross his body and strike the stonework on the other side. He hung on to life until the last second, trying to get the loudhailer up to his lips for some final curse. But it slipped at last out of his dead grasp and fell into the crowd below. In a moment,

Czezny himself dropped to his knees and slid forward off the scaffold and out of the lights.'

Fitzwallace slipped through Micklegate Bar in a police van in the small hours of the next morning. In the back, guarded by two armed soldiers, was Rubinstein. They drove straight to the old Debtor's Prison in the Castle Museum, which Fitzwallace had now made his headquarters. There he was pushed into a small cramped cell that had once held a display of old gunsmiths' tools. Next door, Davidson and Watkin, the two survivors of the St. Martin's Lane Massacre, still lay in the old condemned cell.

'What,' said Rubinstein, standing defiantly in the middle of the cell, 'do you intend should be done with me now?'

'Nothing,' said Fitzwallace.

'This is treason to the cause,' said Rubinstein.

'Not really,' said Fitzwallace. 'The cause is clear enough. We're both working for it. But there is a disagreement over method.'

'Method is embodied in cause,' said Rubinstein.

'No doubt,' said Fitzwallace with a dismissive wave of the hand. 'But war is the happy suspension of philosophy. Your liberalism, your devotion to the sweet reason of the cerebral cortex—these are anathema to action. Tell me this: I broadcast a battle cry last night, a call to Odin and the old gods of the North. I declared the North an independent state at war with the state of London. Would you have allowed that message to go out if I hadn't removed you from office?'

'No,' said Rubinstein. 'So you've brought us to this? To civil war?'

'I've interpreted the spirit of the North and given it action.' He smiled and gave a little bow. 'My dear Rubinstein,' he said, backing out through the cell door.

Upstairs, in what had been the museum curator's room, Wordsworth was waiting. He was in a towering rage. 'You bloody insane swine!' he cried, as Fitzwallace walked in.

'Not now. Not now. There's a great deal to be done.'

Fitzwallace hung up his cap and put his briefcase and sword-stick on the table. He sat down. 'What developments have there been?' he said.

Wordsworth leaned across the table at him. 'You should be shot—shot!' he shouted.

'No doubt,' said Fitzwallace.

'Do you know what you've done?'

'Yes, I know.'

'You've seized power in your own hands without any reference to the Central Committee. Treason and treachery man! Dictatorship! Personal aggrandisement!'

'My dear Sir Brian; you asked me a simple question "did I know what I had done?" I gave you a simple answer—"yes". Do we need to develop the point at length—really? I am authorized by the Council of the North to act in an executive capacity. In Manchester I found a situation that required immediate action. I acted. You say I acted without reference to the Central Committee. I telephoned Olsen and he gave me his support. I telephoned Brunton, but he wasn't available. If he had been, I should have had his support. In the Central Committee that would have produced three votes in support of my decision against your own vote in support of yourself. How have I acted unconstitutionally or undemocratically?'

'I knew nothing about your intentions, nothing! What kind of constitutional action is it that neglects to inform the chairman?'

'Not neglects, Sir Brian. I assure you it was quite deliberate on my part. You've told me how you see my action—a piece of "personal aggrandisement" was it? Seeing it in that way, is it likely that I would have had your support? Hardly. Without your support what should I have done? Neglected to act where I knew action to be essential? Or acted in defiance of your ruling? Be honest; you would have dithered, because you would have been unsure how far advancement of the cause would have detracted from your own personal ambition. Your real objection to the action is that *I* thought of it and *I* executed it—not *you*.'

'You talk of three votes against my one. Aren't you forgetting Rubinstein. Or are you arrogant enough to believe he would have supported you?'

'Rubinstein is no longer on the Central Committee.'

'What! What have you done with him?'

'Really—I'm tired. I've had no sleep for more than twenty-six hours. This melodrama . . . Rubinstein is perfectly fit. You'll have his resignation in a few hours.'

Wordsworth turned and walked back to the window. 'I shall call a meeting of the full Council at once. They can decide between us.'

'Very wise,' agreed Fitzwallace. 'But tomorrow will be too late.' He glanced at his watch. It was a quarter to five. 'It might already be too late.'

6

ONE of Macey's armoured vehicles gave mechanical trouble. On a skeleton raid such as he was engaged in, every piece of equipment was essential. It couldn't be abandoned. In consequence, its repair held up the entire operation for three hours. In effect, it delayed it for one whole day for it meant that instead of arriving on target at 5 a.m., they would have arrived at 8 a.m. when the streets would already be filling with traffic and quick withdrawal would be impossible.

Macey led his column into woods north of High Wycombe at 5.30 that morning, hoping fervently that if they were seen they would be dismissed as part of yet another army manoeuvre. During the morning the men slept, some in the trucks, most amongst the bracken under the trees. Macey himself slept until 10 and then rechecked the plan in the light of the new timing. He was irritable. The old excitement of the previous evening had turned sour because of the delay. He complained about the food served up to him. During the afternoon the men lay about in groups talking, checking their arms and supplies and playing cards. The passage of time seemed to increase rather than diminish Macey's edginess. When two forest workers walked into the camp just after 4 p.m. to ask what was going on, he stormed at them and threatened to have them shot. It was unfortunate. Instead of forgetting the incident they talked about it that evening in a pub in High Wycombe. They were overheard and questioned by a policeman in plain clothes, and through him news of Macey's presence reached the authorities. Later that evening a detachment of the Southern army was moved to the outskirts of High Wycombe ready to move out and investigate in the morning.

As night fell, and the men began to make preparations for a

few hours sleep, Macey's old ebullience returned. The years slipped off him. He felt young again. There was the old sense of freedom and slight irresponsibility that he always experienced as action approached. He walked among the men, chatting to a group here, joking to others there. He had checked earlier that all preparations had been made. There was nothing to do but enjoy the pre-battle sensation and make sure the men got a little sleep. At 10 p.m. he turned in himself.

He was woken at 3 in the morning, by the guard shaking his arm through the open lorry window. He got out of the cab and stretched, then splashed some water over his head and face from a jerry-can. A bird twittered sleepily and in the far distance a cock was crowing. The men were climbing out of the lorries and handing mugs of tea to one another. Porridge and fried eggs and bacon had been prepared on a portable gas range. The smell filled the woods. Everyone felt hungry in that early, crisp air. Macey called his officers to him when he had finished eating, and gave them the last instructions. At 3.30 he climbed into the cab of his lorry and led the way out of the wood and on to the road. He took the route round Amersham and Rickmansworth and reached Western Avenue at Denham, in the full light of the early day. It was already warm. Few vehicles were on the road. The sight of an army convoy so near the capital, drew almost no attention. A motorcycle patrolman waved them through the lights at Hanger Hill and Macey waved his thanks with a laugh. Things, he thought, were going extremely well. He checked his street map. It looked less than a mile now to the target. It was 4.45 a.m. on his watch. He began to sing to himself whilst his driver stared in concentration down the almost empty road ahead.

Wormwood Scrubs prison lay over the rooftops to the left and in a moment they were turning right down Wood Lane, round the corner of the White City Stadium with its flags hanging limp overhead. The vast mast of the BBC TV Centre came into sight and the driver began to slow down. Macey, through the wing mirror on his side, could see the rest of the convoy close behind him. There was a gentle squeak of brakes from somewhere behind. The driver stuck his arm through the window and turned into the main gates of the TV Centre.

A middle-aged man in navy-blue uniform came out of the glass checkpoint and put up a hand, but they drove past him. The lorries drove up to the main building and parked in a continuous line behind one another. Before they had come to a stop men began to drop from them and run up the steps of the building. The light armoured vehicles, last in the convoy, turned once they were inside the gates to cover the entrance with machine guns.

'What's going on?' called the uniformed man from the checkpoint. 'You can't come in here without a pass. No one's told me nothing about you.'

'Exercise,' shouted the commander of an armoured vehicle.

'Why did nobody tell me?'

'Search me.'

'I'll have to check,' said the man, moving back to the checkpoint.

'No need,' called the commander.

'I've my job to think of,' said the man, over his shoulder.

'Shall I, sir?' said Jones on the machine gun.

'Wait,' said the commander, a young lieutenant with a thin, sandy moustache. 'If he touches that phone, hit him.'

Through the glass of the checkpoint everything the man did was visible. He ran his finger down the page of a book, as if looking for some entry that he had missed. Then he turned over the papers in a tray on his table. Finally he peered through the glass again. He saw the armbands with the large letter N. He saw the machine gun pointing in his direction. He saw the troops rushing into the main building and some dim pattern began to coalesce in his mind. He picked up the telephone and began to dial. The burst of machine gun fire shattered the glass in front of him, and he fell out of sight behind the table.

Men took up positions guarding the lorries. Others began to unload equipment and carry it into the building. A party of six men led by a sergeant began to unroll wire from inside the building, down the steps and across to plungers set up behind the cover of the armoured vehicles.

Inside the entrance hall, Macey was directing parties to various parts of the building with tremendous enthusiasm. He carried a Stirling which he waved about in encouragement. Men ran along the empty corridors and up the stairs, carrying boxes of explosives and incendiary material and reeled out wire behind them. Cleaners in the corridors and offices retreated terrified into corners. Some were pushed towards the stairs with warnings about their safety if they didn't hurry outside. Night staff filed out of offices with their hands behind their heads and made for the exits. A videotape editor, working through the night to put the last touches to a rush job, lifted the phone to tell his wife to expect him within the hour and was struck down by a rifle butt. It says a great deal for the degree of surprise that Macey had achieved, that not a single message from the building reached the outside world until all the troops were clear.

A gunner in one of the armoured vehicles standing at the entrance gates, saw billowing white smoke begin to pour from a window on an upper floor. It was followed by a vast cloud of darker smoke ascending from the main body of the building behind the entrance façade. From somewhere deep in the building—it was in fact from No. 1 Studio—came a dull, growling explosion that shattered glass in a dozen windows overlooking the approach area. A man in shirt sleeves appeared at a second floor window and began shouting: 'Fire! Fire!' But as he shouted, smoke billowed up behind him and poured past him through the open window so that he disappeared from view.

Now the whole top of the building seemed alight. An explosion shook a different part of it every few seconds. Troops began to emerge from the main doors and run to the lorries. Drivers were starting up the engines. Macey backed out of the doors towards the steps shouting for the remaining men inside to get a move on. He was scorched all the way up his left side, where he had got too close to an exploding incendiary. He shook his left hand as if it was giving him pain. A man came out, supported by two others. He had lost all his hair and his battledress tunic was still smouldering. 'My bloody hands!' he was screaming.

At each lorry, a man was checking off names on a roll, as men climbed in over the backboards. As each lorry load was accounted for, the man stood by the side of his vehicle with his roll of names held high in the air. Finally, everyone was accounted for, and Macey got into the cab of the leading lorry. Before he had slammed the door behind him, the vehicle began to pull away. The column moved round the perimeter road and back to the entrance gates. The armoured vehicles revved their engines and began to inch forward to join the end of the convoy as it swung back into Wood Lane. As the last of the lorries manoeuvred through the gates and the first of the armoured vehicles began to clatter after it, the officer on the plunger rammed it home. There was a deep, prolonged, rumbling explosion and the whole façade of the building began to crumble and topple. Finally it slid down with a thunderous crash on to the main entrance steps. In a moment a cloud of dust and smoke hid it from view. As the last armoured vehicle pulled into the road, Jones, looking back from his position on the gun, saw the vast transmitting mast tilt and begin to bend.

The convoy turned into West Way, round the corner of the White City Stadium. 'Let's give 'em an encore,' shouted someone in the leading lorry, pointing up at the stadium building. The bells of fire engines could be heard ahead. There were six of them, clattering and swerving through the mounting traffic on the far side of the road. They rattled and clanged towards the convoy without a pause. 'Stand by!' cried the officer in the leading armoured vehicle, and as the fire engines drew level he shouted, 'Now!' The first burst caught the leading engine in the cab and in the tyres. It began at once to slew across the road out of control. It struck a lamp-standard and began to roll over. As it did so, flames flickered out of it and as the second engine struck it, a sheet of burning petrol flared across the road. Two cars, their brakes screaming, tried to avoid the burning mass, but were driven straight into it by the third engine. None of the engines escaped. One ran over the kerb and rammed itself into the front of a house, and the two others, trying desperately to avoid the crash ahead, ran over the central marking in the road and ploughed head-on into traffic moving in the opposite direction. In a moment, both carriageways were closed with wrecked and blazing vehicles and Macey's convoy was clear. Not a soul had any coherent idea of what had happened. It was still not half-past five.

Macey was elated. The tension was released. He sang loudly in the cab. The job was over. Finished. A total success. Three vehicles behind him was a photographer with shots that could prove it. Ahead, there was now only the steady drive north. It was fortunate that despite his elation, despite behaviour that would have appeared to an observer unjustified if not quite irresponsible in the circumstances, his long experience of similar situations left his judgement unimpaired. He chose to continue to pull out to the west, rather than driving north through Wembley and Harrow and picking up the M1 at Watford. It was his intention to keep to the sideroads in the direction of Bicester, Banbury and Coventry, and join the M6 at what used to be the old Gailey roundabout.

When the PM's Defence Committee had pieced together all the detailed information about the raid that reached them, and made of it a coherent if incredible pattern, it was not 6.30 a.m. Within minutes of that time, all roads leading out of London to the north were closed and low-level fighters were patrolling M1 as far as the service area at Newport Pagnell.

It was unfortunate, however, that Macey chose to by-pass High Wycombe a mile or so to the north, for it was there that he met the Southern patrol already searching the woods for him.

News of the destruction of the Wood Lane TV Centre reached the North by way of BBC radio, almost as quickly as it reached the South. When the Council of the North met in the chamber of the City Council in the Guildhall of York, it was naturally confused and disunited. Many of its members were elated that the North had been able to strike such a blow to Southern communications in the very heart of the enemy city. A few repented of their membership of a Council that could be so ostentatiously aggressive. They realized too late, that the negotiations they had been hoping for would never materialize. The harmless ideals of freedom and liberty they had nurtured for so long, had armed themselves during the night. Dragon's teeth. But, approving or disapproving, all were anxious for an explanation of the action and a clarification of the situation.

Fitzwallace might have harnessed the feelings to himself, but he chose quite deliberately to be absent from the meeting. He was up in Newcastle making the final arrangements for the raising of the North-eastern army under Lt. General Quigley. Olsen had agreed to speak for him. Fitzwallace knew that his absence would disquiet Wordsworth, since Wordsworth himself had no more inside facts than most other Council members. He knew, too, that Wordsworth's main attack on him before the Council, would be based on the charge of personal grandeur and dictatorship. Fitzwallace knew that no such charge could be levelled at Olsen. Olsen was too open to appear insincere and not sufficiently competent before such a meeting to appear a demagogue. Olsen, too, was now well briefed with the facts. He could put Fitzwallace's case more effectively than Fitz-wallace himself. Not that Fitzwallace had much to fear from the Council's opposition. He knew he was too firmly in the saddle now. He could, if necessary, put an army against the Council, for he had the support of the Northern military and the vast mass of people.

'I'm not very good at this sort of thing, Mr. Chairman,' began Olsen, armed with a sheaf of notes too large to handle. 'But I think I can tell the Council the facts of what has happened during the last forty-eight hours. As we've seen this morning, it takes some time to call a full meeting of the Council. Most of us are here, but even now I see some absences. Lady Jane Griffith is not with us—and Sir Walter Frankland. To govern by full Council in an emergency like this, would be—well, not really to govern at all. As I understand it, this is why you elected a Central Committee. To make those decisions on your behalf that it was physically impossible for the full Council to take.

'Well, now. If we look at the Central Committee. Mr. Rubinstein is in Manchester and Sir Felix Brunton is in Leeds. In York, which has become the seat of the Council, there are virtually three of us. I should explain that I have moved here for the time being and our chairman lives within a convenient distance. Colonel Fitzwallace, of course, was already living here before our formation. When a sudden crisis came up, of course those of us on the spot knew about it first. Since one of those people was our chairman, and since the three of us were a majority of the Committee, it's natural that we should have taken most of the share in dealing with problems that needed instant decisions.

'This is what happened when Colonel Fitzwallace visited Manchester. He found a situation that demanded instant decision and action. Any delay in acting could have been disastrous. As it is, the action he took has put us in a strong and united position. We now have all the Northern TV transmitting stations entirely at the disposal of the Council. We have destroyed the enemy's principal transmitting station and we have shown him that we have the strength and determination to carry out our aims. I personally think Colonel Fitzwallace was right in authorising this action. I hope that Council will continue to give him its support.'

Wordsworth leaned back heavily in the great oak chair, beneath the pictures of the Lord Mayors of York. He was tapping a pencil on the desk in front of him in irritation. His heavy face was clouded with anger. He had some difficulty in not interrupting Olsen's naïve pronouncement. He was used to Board work and he was used to control. He found it difficult to bear the surprising sense of sympathy and understanding with which the Council took the explanations of this gauche young man. 'Why,' he said, 'did it not occur to Fitzwallace to consult his chairman?'

Olsen turned to him across the intervening seats. 'Well,' he said, 'he rang me from Manchester and he had my support. I suppose he thought that since it had become accepted that the three of us in York should make whatever immediate decisions were necessary, my support would in any case give him a majority.'

'Whatever you imagine has become accepted,' said Wordsworth, 'the fact remains that two is not a majority in a committee of five.'

'He rang Sir Felix Brunton but couldn't get hold of him. But he was sure of his support in an emergency.'

'I've spoken to Sir Felix this morning,' said Wordsworth. 'He tells me that he would never have given his support.'

'Indeed no,' said Sir Felix, looking up with his sad eyes from the notes he had been scribbling.

'And Rubinstein—did he make no attempt to sound Rubinstein? He was after all in Manchester.'

'I'm told that Mr. Rubinstein has resigned from the Central Committee,' said Olsen.

'You are told, are you?' growled Wordsworth. 'By whom?'

'By Colonel Fitzwallace of course.'

'Of course. And where is Rubinstein now? Where is this resignation of his? Nothing has reached me.'

'Well—I imagine it will.'

'No doubt it will,' said Wordsworth, his cheeks shaking with a fury he found it difficult to control.

Stephen Jackman rose from a far seat. 'This really is extremely serious,' he said, in his slow measured manner. 'A member of the Central Committee seems actually to have disappeared. He is supposed to have resigned, yet no resignation has been received by the chairman. We have only the word of one man to go on here, and that man—Colonel Fitzwallace—isn't even present. Could we perhaps have an explanation of his absence, Mr. Chairman?'

'I can give you none,' said Wordsworth. 'Olsen's given me a verbal apology from him, but no explanation.'

'Colonel Fitzwallace is in Newcastle,' said Olsen, running his fingers through his long, dark hair. He began to feel a need to defend Fitzwallace, but was unsure how to go about it. 'There is the question of organizing defences in case of retaliation.'

'But if Colonel Fitzwallace hadn't taken matters into his own hands,' persisted Jackman, grasping the back of the bench in front firmly in both hands, 'there would be no question of retaliation. I say that this action against the South should not have been taken.'

There were a number of cries against him. It was clear that this was not what the majority felt. They were more than satisfied with the action, and despite Wordsworth's questioning of Olsen they were growing more convinced that Fitzwallace had been right in everything he had done.

'Of all the pusilanimous drivel,' snapped Dr. Blackett, turning in his seat to face Jackman. 'The man was given our authority to act for us. He's done no more. What did we put him there for if we expected him to consult us before he made a decision? All this time-wasting squabbling this morning. A fat lot of decisions we'd be able to make. We're in the middle of a war and all you can talk about is etiquette. For the love of God, Chairman, let's move that what Fitzwallace has done has our approval.'

There were cries in support. Half a dozen hands went up. Wordsworth, who would have liked to see Fitzwallace crushed by an avalanche of disapproval, said nothing. He sat stiffly erect in his high-backed chair of office, tap-tapping his pencil on the desk in front of him. To speak against Fitzwallace now would have been to expose himself to the vociferous disapproval of the Council. Worse; it would have been to align himself in everyone's eyes with Jackman. And Jackman and his like were anathema to Wordsworth. It was then that he took the decision to remove Fitzwallace in some other, less constitutional way. The more Fitzwallace grew in authority over these people, the bigger would be the gap left when he went. Into that gap Wordsworth would step, before anyone could oppose him. It would be still simpler if Wordsworth alone knew when the gap was about to be created.

'Very well,' said Wordsworth at last. 'If you'll put that as a motion, Blackett . . .'

York, the ancient capital of the North, began to sense the return of its old status. Old St. John's church in Micklegate, at one time the Institute of Advanced Architectural Studies of the University, became in effect a centre of propaganda, reviving memories of the Viking past with displays and illustrated lectures. Olsen organized a military tattoo on the broad grassy acres of the Knavesmire, to replace the Festival of the Arts which had come so abruptly to an end with the death of Czezny and the internment of all visiting actors and musicians behind the railings of the Museum Gardens. Bands of the Northern regiments—the Green Howards, the KOYLIs, the Northumberland Fusiliers, the Lancashires, the DLIs—pumped out brassy marches. Troops re-enacted the Viking invasions up the river. The battles of Stamford Bridge, bloody Towton and

Marston Moor were refought during the sunny afternoons. Guards patrolled the medieval walls at night and the portcullises of the four ancient entrances into the City were lowered at 11 p.m. The City became again a fortress.

It was before the lowered portcullis of Micklegate Bar, the south-west gateway into the City, that Valerie Paine arrived late on the night of June 5th. Her case had gone. She had lost the heel of one shoe, so that even without the blisters on her feet she would have limped. She had travelled from Retford by taxi, lorry, private car, and on foot, somehow avoiding the tight frontier security and the frequent roadblocks within the North itself. It had taken her more than forty-eight hours. The narrow pedestrian archway to the left of the portcullis was guarded by two soldiers with rifles and fixed bayonets. Behind them a machinegun emplacement had been set up.

'God almighty!' said one of the soldiers when she stepped into the light and he saw the state she was in. 'What the bloody hell's this then?'

'Take me to your commanding officer,' she said, steadying herself with one hand against the stonework of the gateway.

'Not likely,' he said. 'I'd be on jankers for a month.'

'I wish to see Colonel Fitzwallace.'

'Get away!'

'If I don't see your commanding officer at once, I shall suggest to Colonel Fitzwallace that he has you shot,' she said quietly.

The soldier seemed amused but not impressed. 'Well,' he said. 'What authority you got?'

She gave him the only document in her possession that could have impressed him. It was an old letter to her from Fitzwallace, from which she had torn the date. It bore his name, address and personal monogram. It began: 'My own dear Valerie.'

'You will see from this,' she said, 'that I am Colonel Fitzwallace's mistress.'

The guard commander felt that he couldn't ignore the letter. He had her taken by car to Fitzwallace's headquarters in the old Debtors' Prison. Fitzwallace had taken over the building from the Castle Museum authorities and many of the exhibits were still in position in showcases on the walls. He used the entire second floor as his own personal quarters.

Sidney Olsen put out a hand to help her up the staircase. She looked at him for a moment. A look of tired amusement. 'So,' she said at last, 'this is what fame looks like at close quarters.'

'Fame?' said Olsen, his hand still unconsciously held out for her to take.

She took his hand at last and began slowly to climb the staircase. 'Of course—fame,' she said. 'We've even heard of you in town.'

On either side of the corridor leading to Fitzwallace's private drawing room, were collections of arms and displays of Cromwellian armour. Prominently placed in front of one show-case, was an exhibit labelled: 'Copy of the Death Mask of Oliver Cromwell'. She smiled wryly. It was a new angle of Douglas Fitzwallace.

Fitzwallace found her asleep on a Victorian chaise-longue when he returned in the early hours of the next day. He had flown back from Newcastle to Elvington in a B.862 and been driven to York in an armoured saloon. He lifted her gently, but she didn't wake. He laid her in his own bed and drew the covers round her. He didn't undress that night because of the news that was beginning to come in from Macey. In between disconnected dispatches, rumours and occasional messages picked up from the broadcasts of enemy patrols that were coming in, he managed to rest on the chaise-longue in his drawing room. By 6 a.m., the picture that was beginning to emerge of Macey's position, was far from rosy.

Ahead of Macey stood four tracked armoured vehicles. They were light and very fast. Over open, firm ground he might have stood a chance against them. Here, he had no choice but to stop.

'Get that armband off,' he snapped to his driver. 'Keep your gun handy.'

They drew up before the first vehicle and a young lieutenant came up to them. He saluted when he saw Macey's rank. 'Think we're looking for you, sir,' he said.

'Really?' said Macey.

'Were you camped in a wood yesterday, sir—bit north of here?'

'Look here, Lieutenant, we're virtually at war. You know better than to ask that kind of thing without some sort of proof of identity—some authority.'

'Well sir, I've no written authority. But if you care to check with Colonel Ellis in Windsor . . .'

'Let me understand you, Lieutenant. You're suggesting I lead this convoy to Windsor, see this Colonel of yours, and having established your identity and mission, return here to answer your questions, hm?' He gave a laugh of genuine amusement.

'Well, no sir . . .'

'All right, You've your job to do. We're part of *Sea Beagle*—this sea-arm co-op thing. We were in the wood yesterday, but I thought we'd got away without being spotted. But for you we would have done. Good man. We're making for Amersham —perhaps you'd direct us.'

'Certainly, sir. Top of the hill and turn right. It's signposted all the way.'

'I wouldn't be too sure,' laughed Macey.

'And thank you sir,' said the Lieutenant with a crisp salute. 'Sorry to have held you up.'

'All right,' snapped Macey to the driver. 'Move, but steady now.' He gave the Lieutenant a token salute as he passed. More particularly he was noticing the strength of the crews of the four vehicles and the armament. He thought that, given a chance to manoeuvre he could possibly handle them. If he had sufficient warning to set them up, there were the mortars and the anti-tank missiles in the last lorry. As they drew to the top of the hill the driver said, 'Amersham, sir?' 'Don't be a madman,' cried Macey. 'We'd walk straight into it that way. Left—down here. And let her out a bit.' They ran down through woods deep in shade. Macey had his eyes on the map. He wanted the secondary roads and he wanted to confuse any pursuit as much as possible. At the same time, it would have been disastrous to take a road that led nowhere or that was crossed by a bridge too low for the convoy to get under. After six or seven minutes he ordered the driver to pull in to a wide grass verge. He got out and called for Major Edkin.

'My God, sir', said Edkin, brushing up his moustache with the back of his index finger. 'I thought that was it. Nearly on the point of letting rip.'

'Damn good thing you didn't,' said Macey. 'I want you up in front with your car. With luck we'll meet no one. But if we do, then we'll just have to shoot it out. That lieutenant can't be such a damn' fool that he won't radio in as soon as he gets a chance. Then of course they'll know where we are. I'm banking on 'em still thinking we must go north. Well we're not. Not for a hell of a lot of miles. Tell everyone that if we get jumped then they're on their own. Get the hell out of it quick as they can. We're not stopping to fight. No damned heroics—hm? Rendez-vous if possible here—' he pointed to a crossroads north-east of Newbury '—at 09.00. Wait fifteen minutes—no more. If things get really rough then I'm making for Gloucestershire—maybe even Wales. I'll get a message through to HQ as soon as I can. Can't risk it yet though. They'll be listening like hawks. Good luck!'

One of the armoured vehicles clattered to the front, and Macey pulled out behind it. Ahead and behind he had placed motor-cycle outriders. He was still not sure that he had made the right decision. In theory, there was more chance of escape if he split up the convoy. On the other hand, his present force could handle the average patrol without difficulty. And there was at the back of his mind the gambler's instinct that told him the Southern patrol's report might not be linked with the London raid. Well, it was a chance, though a slim one. He had committed himself to it.

Less than twenty minutes after the encounter with the Southern patrol, the forward outrider drew up by the side of Macey's lorry to report the approach of two helicopters from the north. They were combing the roads from a height of five hundred feet. From the shelter of a wood Macey and his men heard them approach, chop-chopping over the trees. Their shape couldn't be made out clearly, because of the denseness of the foliage, but as they crossed the sun they cast shadows over the morning. They slid away, swung back again directly overhead, and finally clattered off to the south.

Macey called his officers together. 'Difficult to cover ourselves against air attack if it comes,' he said. 'We're breaking up. I want two units with an armoured vehicle each. Move independently. Like this we'd be dog food for the fighter-bombers. Try to stay together. That way you'll have more chance with roadblocks and ground patrols. If things get too hot, get off the road and lie low until dark. If you have to, ditch the vehicles and move on foot.' He stabbed at the map with his finger: 'Try to get here, east of Gloucester, by midnight. I'll wait in this wood until 02.00 hours, then I'll push west into Wales. Better mark the place on your maps. Tomorrow night I should be here, west of Chester. I'll put a man at this crossroads for twenty-four hours, then I'll move back to base. You might listen out at noon tomorrow. If things have eased, I'll send a signal to HQ.'

The helicopters dogged Macey for an hour. He lost a lot of time by having to get off the road every time they were reported. Near Stokenchurch they were concentrating in the next small valley. This time they had something pinned down. They turned round and round over one particular spot, not moving forward at all. Within minutes, four fighter-bombers had appeared from the south and the helicopters climbed out of the way. Macey, his lorries under the cover of overhanging trees by the roadside, watched through binoculars from the ridge. Nothing moved in the valley, and however carefully he searched the woods and cover, he could make out nothing. But the fighter-bombers dropped down and opened up on the valley bottom with rockets and machineguns. Finally they came in with their bombs. Huge columns of earth and dust flew into the air, and the din of the explosions reverberated across the valley. Macey saw the dense black smoke of burning fuel begin to rise from behind the woods. There was a dull, long explosion. The aircraft turned twice over the scene, and then slid away to the south. 'Well,' said Macey to the lieutenant commanding the armoured vehicle, 'it wasn't all of us at any rate.'

There were signs of aircraft activity throughout the morning.

It was gone noon before Macey crossed the Newbury-Abingdon road south of Steventon, and a little before three-thirty they caught him north-east of Marlborough. The outrider was a mile ahead of the main body. He was cut down by fire from the helicopter as it spun round from the corner of a wood. They had him in sight for some minutes, picking him up by the light wisp of dust he threw up from the surface of the crumbling road. Before the main vehicles reached him, the fighter-bombers were on them. There were two of them. The first Macey knew of it was the shattering explosion ahead and to the right. The windscreen shattered and glass struck his face. The driver rolled over on to him, blood covering his face. His leg was locked hard down on the accelerator. The lorry swerved to the left. Macey tried to get past the driver's body to push over the wheel, but as his hands grasped it they were off the road, rolling over and ploughing deeply along a ditch. Macey's position, below the level of the road and wedged beneath the body of the driver, saved him from the machinegun bullets as the fighters made a second run. He heard something explode further back on the road and smoke and fumes of burning fuel began to fill the cab. He waited. He thought he had escaped unhurt. The blood on him seemed to be coming from the driver. He lay there until he heard the sound of the aircraft fade and finally disappear beyond detection. There was only the steady crackle of flames from somewhere behind, and occasionally the crack of exploding ammunition.

He pushed the driver forward against the smashed windscreen and got clear of him. He got out at last through the windscreen and found himself on his hands and knees in the ditch bottom. It was damp and smelt foul in the hot afternoon. He stood up in it and put his hand to his face. He was bleeding badly where the glass had struck him. Peering over the top of the ditch, he saw the second lorry blazing just behind him. There was no sign of life from it. He could see the bodies of the two men still in the cab behind the flames. The fourth lorry had run off the road on the far side and the third seemed to have disappeared altogether. Up in the sky nothing moved. All was quite again. He climbed to the road.

The armoured vehicle, when they came to inspect it, was

still serviceable. The third lorry was wedged firmly between two old haystacks. The driver had seen the fighters a second before they struck, and run through an open gateway into a field. The gap between the haystacks had looked in that second a God-given bolthole. The armoured vehicle, slewing and skidding on the earth, dragged them clear. By cannibalizing the two forward lorries which were beyond recovery, they managed to get the fourth one back on the road. But it took them forty minutes and during that time Macey expected at any moment to see a ground patrol appear to investigate. They laid the dead—there were more than twenty of them—gently on the grass verge. Macey packed the more severely wounded into one of the remaining lorries and ordered them to give themselves up to the first troops or police they came across in Marlborough. Then, with one lorry, one light armoured vehicle, and less than twenty-five men, he continued to move west. He reached cover at the rendezvous east of Gloucester at 8 in the evening. Macey issued cold rations, then the men got under the trees and slept. No one spoke. By 2 in the morning, no one else had kept the rendezvous. Macey was depressed and irritable. He spoke to no one, except to give the briefest of orders, and no one felt like approaching him. Three minutes before he left cover, he decided to risk the briefest of signals. It said: 'Mission successful. Withdrawal tough. Position 7a towards 5.'

7

VALERIE PAINE woke at 10 o'clock with the sun streaming in through the windows. The room was large and high, painted a shabby green from floor to ceiling. On the walls were arrays of arms and yellowing oils of no particular distinction. For a moment she had no idea where she was. She felt hot and uncomfortable. When she threw back the coverings of the bed, she found she was still fully dressed. He shoes were at the side of the bed. She put them on, ran her hands along the sides of her head in an automatic gesture to set her hair in place, and then went to one of the two doors leading from the bedroom. 'Hello,' she called, at first tentatively and then more firmly.

'Ah!' cried Fitzwallace from some room beyond. 'Our guest awakes.'

'Guest—or prisoner?' she asked when he came in.

He took her hands and kissed them both. 'My dear Valerie,' he said. 'What a most ungracious question. You have my bed, my room. Your breakfast will be brought to you in a moment. I shall provide toothbrush, toothpaste, comb, hairbrush—all the necessaries of a beautiful woman's toilet. You may stay forever if you wish. And yet you can ask such a question. You have lost both taste and judgement by your long absence from the North—and from myself.'

She laughed. 'Very pretty,' she said. 'But I must be honest with you Douglas . . . '

'Not now,' he said. 'Not before you've eaten. In any case you were always at your most unattractive when you were being honest.'

'You're almost the only man I've been honest with.'

'I'm both flattered and depressed,' he said. 'Come. I'll show you where you can bathe. Primitive as yet. Forgive us—it used to be a museum. The bath has been in only a day or two. Ignore it if it gurgles.' He led the way to a small room beyond his drawing room. On a table were boxes of clothes and toilet materials. Beyond a further door was the bathroom, with lengths of copper piping still stacked in one corner. 'Everything, I hope, that you need for the moment.'

'Oh, Douglas . . .' she said.

'Not a word,' he said bending and kissing her cheek. 'The North and everything it can provide, is open to you.'

Lying immersed in the hot water, she felt elated—excited—by the situation in which she found herself. It had the drama and tension she loved. It had a man she had admittedly once loved and whom she still found fascinating and intriguing. The fact that Robert knew where she was—perhaps even approved—took away scarcely any of the savour. She wondered whether she still had any power over Fitzwallace. At one time she had—two years ago in Oslo. That wonderful month. But everything shifts and changes and passes. Even that. She lifted her breasts in her hands so that the nipples just broke the surface of the water. And nothing, she thought, can ever be repeated. Nothing can ever be the same again. To put back the clock. To crystallize time for ever, so that the chosen moment is the enduring now, so that nothing of mutability ever again impinges on it. She thought of a world of perfumed sensuality in which the day of reckoning never came.

'I never heard from you,' he said as she sat down to breakfast. 'Whatever have you been doing?'

'I wrote last, if you remember,' she said.

'That card on my birthday,' he said. 'That gory reminder? And then a few gossipy pieces about your doings in Nice or Edinburgh—hardly news for my ears.'

'Life,' she said, 'has moved on you know. A few moments of excitement splashed here and there—mostly interminably dull.'

'Dull!' he cried. 'I can hardly believe it. With Paine doing so well, so close to the PM—plumb in the middle of things. Don't you feel a kind of involvement in the great affairs of state?'

'You mustn't be rude about poor Robert,' she said. 'He is reliable and sound—and you are not. I'd find him entirely endurable if I weren't his wife.'

'Still the need for excitement, is that it? And poor old hard-working Paine so humdrum. If he were on my side, I should give him the most thankless and repetitious job I could find. He's the only man I've ever met who wouldn't fall down on it. But you, my dear—how different. You've something of my temperament. Excitement—change—the things that give common humanity ulcers—the life-blood of us both. Your expedition here, through all the barriers and roadblocks, past a dozen guards thinking of making the most violent approaches to you. You could have been shot at any moment, you know. You are the most courageous, reckless creature I've ever met. The most beautiful too. Which of our many secrets do you want to know—and how do you propose getting the information back to the South?'

'You can't really believe—?' She laughed. But he had caught her and she knew he knew it. It was a ridiculous pretence in any case. 'I came out of the sheerest boredom,' she said.

'I don't doubt it,' he said. 'But I wonder if you were entirely wise. More appears to be happening in London at the moment, than up here. I happened to hear the Southern news earlier. Can you believe it, some uncultured villains have burnt the BBC TV Centre to the ground? Now imagine the excitement if you'd been a prisoner in Wormwood Scrubs. What can we do to match that up here. Historically we have some points of interest. But socially we live in a very dull little town.'

'I don't believe it,' she said. 'It can't be true.'

'I have a signal from the man who did it,' said Fitzwallace. He took a paper from his pocket and read the first two words: ' "Mission successful", he says.'

'Then you really mean business—I mean, you really mean war?'

'Surely no one in the South doubts it? I was sure we'd made the situation entirely clear. I think you can take it they'll be a little clearer about it now.'

Wordsworth knew that whatever accident befell Fitzwallace, he must not in any way be associated with it. He could have hired mercenaries, but mercenaries are two-edged. If they accept payment to do a job, they will accept payment to talk about it. He could have found a disgruntled farmworker or two on his own land, who would have been willing to help on the promise of their own farm to work. But a disgruntled man, acting for some ulterior motive, was no more reliable than the mercenary. He needed a man who would act out of principle and conviction, a man to whom payment would have seemed like an attack on his integrity. He thought that he had found such a man in Stephen Jackman. His confrontation of Fitzwallace during the St. Martin's Lane massacre, was widely known. His opposition to Fitzwallace's hard, inflexible line, had been declared too openly and too often for anyone to be unaware of it. He was a man of absolute integrity, a man of rigid principle, a man who had only to be won over to act. Wordsworth gave him dinner in the old Yorkshire Gentleman's Club adjoining Lendal Bridge in York. The title alone, thought Wordsworth, would appeal to his sense of decency and lend an air of respectability to the conversation.

When the meal was over, Wordsworth brushed his mouth and moustache with the stiffly starched serviette and leaned forward so that his stomach pushed at the table. 'I invited you,' he said, deliberately, 'because I think a crucial moment of decision faces us. In your view, what is the function—the aim—of the Council of the North? You can speak quite freely.'

'I'm quite clear about it,' said Jackman, stressing every word with a nodding movement of his head. 'It should be striving to bring a measure of fair play to the North. We've had a bad deal, a very bad deal. That must be put straight.'

'This by force of arms if necessary?'

'If necessary.'

'Hm,' said Wordsworth, as if considering the statement. 'Yes. Quite right. I agree. In principle, of course I agree with you. But what about the practice?' He put up a finger to attract the attention of a waiter.

'Ah,' said Jackman. 'No. I don't agree with the practice. I voted against Fitzwallace at the full Council, not because I disagree with the need for force, but because I disagree—

profoundly disagree—with the way in which it's being used and the purpose for which it's being used.'

'Perhaps there is more agreement between us than I suspected,' said Wordsworth. 'You'll have a brandy?'

'Well,' said Jackman. 'Very kind of you.'

'Two,' said Wordsworth, without turning his head to face the waiter.

'*Remy Martin*, sir?'

'What I usually have,' said Wordsworth.

'This ambition,' Jackman went on. 'This is anathema to me. I'll fight with as much determination as anyone for principles of freedom and liberty. I'll fight for equality. I'll fight against our position in the North as that of second-class citizens, second-rate people. But I will not fight to replace one central government that cares nothing for us, by the central government of one man absorbed in his own importance.'

'Hm,' said Wordsworth. 'You like the brandy?' He rolled his own drink round in the glass, watching it critically in the lights of the room.

Jackman picked up his glass and took a drink. 'Very good,' he said.

'And what are you going to do about it—this ambition?'

'I shall continue to oppose it by every constitutional method open to me. It's not a dead issue. I shall raise it again before the full Council.'

'Constitutional,' said Wordsworth, as if trying to savour the word as he would a claret before passing judgement on it. 'Isn't there a precedent for this, somewhere in the classics? You're a classicist. Isn't there something about Julius Caesar that has a moral for us here? The Shakespeare version?'

Jackman stared at the glass on the table in front of him. He turned it slowly with his fingertips, as if he could see in it some clouded answer to the question. Finally he nodded in his slow, deliberate way. 'It may come to that,' he said.

London opinion burned against the North when the full facts of the destruction in Wood Lane became known. No government could have withstood the pressure from the City for immediate and massive retaliation. News reaching the City later in the day, that the raiding force had been 'wiped out to a man' increased rather than diminished the pressure. There was a feeling that the whole handling of the situation had been far too lenient. 'Who the hell do these peasants think they are?' cried an irate journalist down the bar of the *Salisbury* in the early evening. 'It's time we taught the bastards a lesson.' It represented the feeling of most people in London that evening.

During the day, there had been a meeting of the Defence Chiefs in number 2 committee room. Television cameras and film units had been active throughout the morning, recording the coming and going of Ministers and officials, military leaders and trade unionists. Ambassadors of most European countries, including the USSR, had visited the Foreign Office. The American ambassador had lunched with the Foreign Secretary. The CIGS had been called to number 10 on four separate occasions before 5 in the evening.

Evening passed into night. The PM appeared before the TV cameras of ITN, grave and drawn. He stated the facts simply and concluded with the words: 'We cannot escape the grave and deeply disquieting fact that a state of war exists between those loyal to the crown and those supporting the rebel North.'

Night passed into a grey morning. The summer weather had gone. A light rain fell. The activity was ceaseless still. The BBC put out a great deal of light music on its radio transmitter, interrupting from time to time to review the latest developments in the situation. Massive troop movements were reported throughout the South-east. By evening, long miles of convoys were moving north along M1, A1, A5 and A6. Ahead of them, patrols were trying to define the North by discovering the first lines of hard resistance. Aircraft flew sporadic sorties, severely hampered by the poor weather, spotting the movements of Northern troops and making occasional attacks on forward roadblocks. Zephyrs of the City of Leeds squadron met PV 92s of the County of London squadron over Buxton, but the weather made any decisive contact impossible.

The North, having taken the initiative, needed to move at a less feverish speed. Forward troops were already established in well prepared positions. Aircraft had been on full alert for three days. All squadrons had been engaged in intensive battle training. Massive reserves were already in position. The main body of the forces in the North-west, under General Sir Wilson Smith, had already established its headquarters in Bolton. Large concentrations of men and equipment were moving down A1 from the North-east, under the command of General Lionel Quigley. The effective line of the Northern army, on that damp June evening, ran from Runcorn on the Mersey to Immingham on the Humber through Wilmslow, Chapel en le Frith, Worksop, Retford and Gainsborough.

The definition of the North remained as elusive as ever. Southern patrols moving north parallel to the main convoy routes, had expected to be received with a certain enthusiasm north of London, as the saviours of the South against the Northern barbarians. But they met no enthusiasm anywhere. Indeed, as far south as Bedford and Biggleswade, there was an atmosphere of hostility towards them. Outside Kettering, a group of young people were carrying a banner which read: LONDON GO HOME. A mile north of Preston, between Uppingham and Oakham, a patrol was held up for twenty minutes by railway lines laid across the road. To Paine, a Northerner by birth, the developing picture that he pieced together from all the signals and reports that reached him, was profoundly disturbing. It became increasingly clear to him that what he had suspected but never expressed, was in fact true. The North was not a geographical location, clearly bounded by this river and that range of hills. The North was a attitude, a feeling, a particular philosophical conviction. As such it could exist as easily in Plymouth and Norwich as in Newcastle. It was this fact that took Fitzwallace to Wales in the late afternoon of June 6th, in response to a signal from Macey.

At the Welsh border Macey had found roadblocks and gun emplacements. He was tired. He had had little sleep since the drive south from Manchester. He felt he was beginning to get old. The further he pulled away from the South-east towards the mid-Welsh border, the more his concentration relaxed. He began to doze, his head resting on his folded battledress blouse propped against the frame of the cab. When he woke the driver was shaking him vigorously. They had come to a stop. In front was a roadblock of deep wire. On either side were substantial gun emplacements of sandbags. 'Of all the damn' fools,' muttered Macey, cursing himself. He had let himself be driven straight into the enemy defences.

They put him in a Landrover with a driver and two men behind with automatic rifles. No one spoke to him. When he reached for a cigar in his top pocket, he was prodded sharply from behind with the muzzle of a gun. It was damp outside and misty. The vehicle was draughty. Now that it was all over he felt cold and dejected. In all his experience he had never let himself be taken so easily. Out of habit, he began to inspect the fastening of the door and calculate his chances of escape in that countryside if he were to roll through the open door. In the mirror, when he craned his head over to the right, he could see the two men behind watching him all the time. He wouldn't have the slightest chance.

They travelled for twenty minutes, through rolling wooded country. Along the road, from time to time, Macey saw evidence of troop and transport concentrations. They pulled into the yard of a farm on the left and Macey got out. Inside, he was led through a large, bare kitchen set up as an operations room. Beyond, in what must have been a drawing room, a man in uniform sat alone at a table. He was short and dark-haired. He got up as Macey came in, and seized him by the hand. 'Congratulations,' he cried fervently. 'Magnificent. Gower—my name. Welsh Independence Fighters. We've listened to all their news broadcasts. What a panic! Tell me— how did it burn? Beautiful—beautiful no doubt. I can see it— woosh! Magnificent! Sit down.'

'I don't understand,' said Macey. 'All these preparations going on . . .'

'No?' said Gower, hopping about the room with excitement. 'We're ready to join you. The entire country. We shall strike from the west. Halford Thomas is in Newport ready to give the signal at this moment. Think—after all these years!'

'Well for God's sake!' said Macey, with a bellow of laughter. 'To think of that. I thought I'd walked into one of their damned patrols.'

'Friends—allies. Your allies. Comrades!' cried Gower, now behind the table.

'But you can't just march like that,' roared Macey.

'Why not?' snapped Gower. 'You think we can't?'

'Course you can if you want to. But wouldn't it be better if your friends knew first?'

'They'll know soon enough. They'll hear the noise in Newcastle as we march down Piccadilly.'

'And suppose we're marching down Regent Street—what happens when we meet you outside Swan and Edgar's?'

'We embrace!' He threw his arms wide open. 'Embrace!'

'Let me send a signal,' said Macey. 'They're expecting one at noon. Let me tell them to expect your support.'

'I am not in command, you know—except in this sector. It's not up to me.'

'Oh my God!' said Macey in exasperation. 'Signal your HQ. Get somebody's permission.'

Olsen had an office below the personal suite of rooms that Fitzwallace had made his headquarters. From his window at the back of the building, he looked out on an unbroken expanse of stone wall that formed part of the old Castle of York. By mid-afternoon, it grew so dark that he had to work under artificial lights. The rain struck the parapet of the wall outside and trickled down the pointing between the stones. He was dictating instructions into a small tape-recorder when the guards brought in Valerie Paine.

'Ah,' he said, waving the guards outside. 'Mrs. Paine.'

'Valerie Paine,' she said, sitting down before he could invite her to do so.

'Valerie Paine then. Olsen—Sidney Olsen. If you'll excuse me a moment . . .' He picked up the microphone and spoke a few final instructions into it. Then he put it down and switched off the machine. He rang a bell and in a moment a girl came in and took away the reel of tape.

'I should like to be quite clear about my position,' said Valerie. 'I take it I'm a prisoner. Why am I here—some sort of interrogation?'

'Well no,' said Olsen. 'Good heavens—why should we do that? Colonel Fitzwallace is extremely busy. There's a great deal for him to do. He thought that I might look after you better than he can for the moment. There's no question of imprisonment. You're a guest, really.'

'Then I'm quite free?'

'Quite free. That is—'

'Well?'

'Well, shall I say you're as free as the rest of us. I mean, with a war going on no one's entirely free.'

She saw that she embarrassed him a little. When she looked him full in the eyes, tiny spots of pink appeared on his cheek-bones. It amused her to see his discomfort. 'Entirely free,' she said, watching him as he moved rather gauchely about the room. 'Then I'm free to call you Sidney?'

'If you like,' he said after a moment.

'I'm afraid it really is the most unattractive name. Have you never thought of changing it?'

'No—I'm hardly to blame for it. It's always been a perfectly satisfactory name.'

'For the everyday business, I suppose, of living in the North. But for civilized society I should have thought something like Rodney or Tarquin—Frederick even, has a certain style. But Sidney, now. It has a certain plum pudding centre, don't you think?' Her intention was not to be rude as such. Rather she was sticking pins into carefully selected parts of him to see how he would react. For she found developing in her head a new and interesting project. The more the toyed with it, the more it pleased her, for she could justify its development within the terms of reference given her by the PM. But more important to her than that: it would give her a power over her sometime lover, the disarming, the gallant, the insufferable Colonel Fitzwallace.

'I don't really see why you should be so rude,' said Olsen. 'What have I done that's upset you?'

'Rudeness?' she said, mock horror in her eyes. 'My dear Sidney, how can you mistake innocent, civilized chatter for rudeness? Really—ask yourself—am I in a position to be rude? I'm a prisoner, whatever you say. I'm a stranger in your town. I'm entirely dependent on your kindness for all the necessaries of life. You're too sensitive. I should have realized it. But you looked so strong and authoritative, sitting there when I came in—perhaps unconsciously I was trying to defend myself do you think? But if I've embarrassed you in any way . . . Really, this is a very bad start to our relationship.' She got up and went over to where he was standing fingering the switches on the tape-recorder. 'It's a relationship, you know, that might have to last the duration of the war, since neither of us can break away from it. Let's start again, right from the beginning. I shall call you Mr. Olsen, if that's what you'd prefer. Now—if you'd be kind enough to tell me where I'm to stay . . .'

'Why, yes,' he said. 'It's just across the corridor.'

She smiled. 'I'm glad, I shall be able to keep a sisterly eye on you. And perhaps—if you don't think I'm altogether brazen —we might have dinner together this evening?'

'Well, of course,' he said. 'But I'm eating in here, if that's all right? There might be phone calls, you know—anything. I can't really go out.'

'And it really will be all right if I join you? I don't want to be in the way.'

'Quite all right. Yes of course. I'm sorry—you know?' He made a gesture with his hands. There was a touch of despair about it.

'Of course. Really, I was simply teasing. Silly of me. I get bored at times. I didn't know why Colonel Fitzwallace had got rid of me. I shouldn't have taken it out on you. I'm sorry as well—really.' Across the corridor he stood with the door of her room open for her. She put the flat of her hand on his chest, as if she was quite unconscious of the movement, and said: 'Is there anywhere that I could get a bottle of wine for us? Sort of celebration of my arrival in the North?'

'I'll have something brought in,' he said. 'About seven-thirty?'

'Seven-thirty.'

'I'll call.'

'I'll be ready. And do you mind if we stick to Sidney?'
'After all you said?'
'Now you're teasing *me*.'
'All right,' he said with a smile. 'Sidney, if you want.'
'And Valerie,' she said.
'Valerie.'
She smiled to herself as she closed the door. It was a secret, inward smile that would scarcely have shown to an outsider. But it was nonetheless a smile.

General Sir Maxwell Howard, in command of the 1st Southern Army, had drastically to revise his view of the situation as he drove further north. The active hostility that his men increasingly encountered, was a factor that no one had anticipated. He had expected a clear drive as far, at least, as Bawtry. Beyond that he had expected a clearly defined line of wire, roadblocks and all the other rusting paraphernalia of formal warfare. On one side would be what he described as 'loyalists', and on the other 'damned rebels'. But through Nottinghamshire and northern Lincolnshire, resistance stiffened sharply. In places it had to be broken by force of arms. The villages of Bradmore and Normanton, on the approach roads to Nottingham, had to be decimated by artillery fire before Howard's men could get through them. The 50th Division, making for M1 through Stapleford, found that the crossing of the Trent at Wilford was heavily defended. Later during the evening and night, patrols reported defences ringing the whole city of Nottingham. The advance of the 50th Division came to a standstill. Howard could have advanced round the city, leaving it an island of defiance. But his brief was to crush rebel resistance in the North. Whatever the North was by definition, this unquestionably was resistance. He strutted back and forth under the hurricane lanterns that lit the barn that he had made his temporary headquarters, and issued his orders. He was short, lean and weatherbeaten in appearance, crisp and curt in manner. 'We shall make an example of these people,' he said, sounding as if he took the opposition as a personal affront.

'Our retaliation will be massive. Those who survive it will link the word Nottingham with Falaise and Stalingrad.'

During the next day, the whole of Howard's advance stopped. When it became known that Nottingham was to be the immediate target for a full-scale attack, many of his Midlanders deserted. A few entered Nottingham with news of the attack. Many fled to the north and east, jettisoning their equipment as they went. Dozens were caught and shot. All the time, artillery was being dragged into position round the city and ammunition wagons were taking up their positions at specially selected points. Observers in Arnold could see the array of rocket launchers being set up on the rising ground to the north. Summerfield, chairman of the Citizens Defence Committee meeting in the Vice Chancellor's Lodge of the University, said: 'It's obvious what these swine intend. They want total capitulation under a massive bombardment. They expect to walk through our dead without the loss of a man.' It was in fact very much what Howard had in mind.

Dawn came, clear and bright, on June 7th. In the fields round the waiting guns, larks dropped twittering on to their nests. The late cocks crowed from the middens. Yet, despite the normal sounds of nature, the air was quiet. Quiet and brooding. There was a sense of human concentration. A sense of tension and waiting. Hands were on the lock of the cage where the dark amorphous beast prowled. Hands were at that moment still in control. A reason of sorts still prevailed.

Then, from deep in the south came the dull drum of aircraft. The citizens, lodged in slit trenches in gardens, crouched behind sandbag emplacements on public playing fields, looked up. The men in steel helmets, standing beside the rocket launchers and fieldpieces, looked up. To the south, beyond the river, beyond Ruddington, perhaps beyond Loughborough even, there was a single dark, flat cloud. It grew as the sound grew. As it grew it split into a hundred separate points of darkness against the fresh and lovely sky. Officers with the gun crews raised their binoculars. Some laughed. Most stood in awe. Citizens pushed their children deeper into the slit trenches and shelters. Older children were noticeably pale. The younger ones cried as they felt the anxiety of parents without understanding it. Howard stood on top of a tank outside Edwalton, hands on hips, peering into the southern sky. 'A little softening up should take the edge off their appetites,' he said with satisfaction.

They were Devastators of 35 Group, vast four-engined machines flying in tight boxes of eighteen. They passed over the first artillery formations at 2,000 feet, shattering the air and causing the ground to tremble. The men at the guns put their hands over their ears and lowered their heads instinctively. Howard lifted his glass and saw the first box drop three hundred tons of high explosive and incendiary on Beeston. Slow mushrooms of smoke and debris rose into the air, and then the long reverberating chaos of the explosions burst on the listening ears. The second box of eighteen aircraft was now overhead, turning very gently to the east. In a moment columns of smoke and dust rose from West Bridgford, and as they clung in the air, again there was the shattering clamour of explosions. The air seemed full of the vast drumming machines and the violence of explosions.

Ken Hodgson, deputy firechief, was directing his men by phone and radio from the new fire tower above Upper Parliament Street. By the time the fourth box of aircraft had struck Carlton, the pattern of the attack was clear to him. 'Christ Jesus Almighty,' he cried, his voice out of control and tears running down his cheeks. 'It's the suburbs. All those people still in bed. The kids—women . . . No, God! God listen—it can't be true—God have mercy on them, God have mercy on them, God have mercy on them. In the name of humanity . . .' But there was no mercy. Neither prayers nor cries in the name of humanity could stop them. In fifteen minutes it was over. Six thousand tons of bombs had smashed the living areas of a great city. Whole streets of houses stood in gaping ruins. Buildings that were not entirely shattered were in flames. Streets were blocked with rubble and smouldering woodwork. Fractured gasmains caught fire. Water poured from fissures in the road. In Arnold where tremendous damage had been done, there was no gas, no electricity and no water. Sewage seeped into the streets. Thousands had been caught in their beds; the first intimation they had had of the attack was the sight of their house wall slipping out of sight. Men staggered into consciousness to find their wives dead in bed next to them and their children trapped screaming in the flames upstairs. Hundreds ran bewildered in the streets. Grown men who had built themselves up over the years into mature, responsible members of society, unshakable pillars in the world of business or the professions, screamed and wept in the blazing streets without knowing it. And yet, despite the appalling destruction and chaos, there were pockets of human compassion. At the corner of James Street and Furlong Street, a woman sat in her nightdress on the kerb supporting a man in her arms. He had lost both legs. He was dying. She had never met him before, but surrounded by all that horror she held him to her until the last breath had left him. In Brookfield Road, a man looking for his children stopped to comfort two others who were weeping over the shattered body of their mother.

General Sir Maxwell Howard was explaining his tactics to Lieutenant Fordyce, a pale young man with a burn scar down his left cheek. He drew a rough circle on the ground with his cane and said: 'We can visualize the city as a dartboard. There are two areas at which we might strike. Here, on the periphery of our dartboard we have the "doubles", where a strike counts for twice as much as it would do further towards the centre. That's one area. And the second is here—at the very centre, the bullseye. You have seen us strike at the periphery, Lieutenant. Why do you think that was?'

'I imagine, sir, that this is the factory area. Striking at the means of production.'

'What do you mean by that phrase—the means of production?' snapped Howard, slapping his leg with his cane. The Lieutenant could tell that whatever answer he gave it would be the wrong one.

'Well—the plant, machinery; the factories, sir,' said the Lieutenant.

'Old fashioned thinking, Lieutenant,' said Howard, almost before the Lieutenant had finished speaking. 'Not fundamental enough. Like Marx—communist, you know. The question is, where do the factories come from? Do they just grow, Lieutenant?'

'Well, sir, they're built.'

'And by whom?'

'People, sir,'

'People! Precisely. People. People are the means of production. War is about people, Lieutenant, not things; not machines and factories. People. Know thine enemy, Lieutenant. He is a man, not a machine. Seek him out. Catch him in his bed. Destroy him. Now—you understand the pattern of the bombardment you've just seen, don't you?'

'Yes sir,' said the Lieutenant. He had a nagging idea that there was a fallacy in the argument somewhere. How fundamental had one to be in considering military tactics? If the question 'where do the factories come from' was pertinent, was it not pertinent to ask where the people came from? Which meant adding to Howard's statement that 'war is about people', the rider that war is also about God.

'And now,' said Howard, turning away from the young man, 'we shall wait for estimates of the damage. At 07.00 hours we shall strike at the bullseye.'

Spotting aircraft flying over the smouldering wreck of the suburbs, reported massive damage. Fires raged and thick palls of smoke made aerial photography difficult. At 7 a.m. the artillery barrage opened with the woosh of rockets spinning upwards from their launching platforms. Helicopters, hanging in the air a mile or two from the target area, reported strikes throughout the city centre. Then, from every point on the city's periphery, came the deep crump of the fieldguns. Shells screamed over the suburbs adding to the panic there, and crashed down Clumber Street and into the area of Victoria Station. Fine new blocks of buildings that had taken years to plan, to be approved, to be financed and built, slid down and across the streets. The new fire tower dropped in a cloud of dust and flying rubble as its first floor was chopped out by blast. Ken Hodgson, the deputy firechief, dropped a hundred and fifty feet to his death. The whole of Goldsmith Street ceased to exist. The new Playhouse, where they were due to rehearse *Richard III* later in the morning, sank amongst its own rubble.

In York, at Northern headquarters, vague messages had been

coming through from radio broadcasts within the besieged city. No one could doubt what was happening. But in the absence of Fitzwallace in Wales, no one seemed able to make any sweeping decision. The fact was they took too narrow a view of the situation. They thought in terms of the North finishing at their own front lines. It had not occurred to anyone that Nottingham would stand alone and isolated and offer such fierce resistance. Wordsworth, with his essential parochialism, refused to send help on the strength of a few disjointed pieces of radio conversation. General Quigley, commanding the Northumbrian Army, advised Wordsworth to wait for more definite news. 'At the moment,' he said, 'we're sitting in impregnable positions. If we move out on the strength of rumours, we could be caught and crushed.' Olsen, anxious to send any help that was possible, lacked the force to overrule Wordsworth. As a compromise, it was agreed to send four Zephyrs to reconnoitre. They reported that Nottingham was in flames and that Howard's men had completely surrounded the city. At the same time, a firm radio message was received from the city. It finished: 'In the name of Christ, help us.'

Venturers from Linton-on-Ouse, covered by two squadrons of Zephyrs, began to attack Howard's artillery at 7.25 a.m. They did considerable damage, destroying rocket launchers, heeling the big field pieces on to their sides. But it was too late. The city had died. The centre was a shattered mass of broken buildings and crushed vehicles. A thousand dead lay in the rubble round the *Victoria* in Milton Street, and from the air no life could be seen in the suburbs. At 9 a.m. jubilant Southern troops marched into the ruins behind a brass band playing 'Maybe It's because I'm a Londoner', pillaging, looting, bayoneting survivors. Howard's plan for massive retaliation had been totally successful. His boast: 'I shall destroy this town without the loss of a man', had almost literally come true.

8

POLITICALLY, the decimation of Nottingham was disastrous. There had been doubts in the North about the wisdom of the freebooting raid on the BBC TV Centre in the minds of many influential Northerners. Jackman's attitude to Fitzwallace's leadership was typical of that of many people. But when the full news of what Howard had done to Nottingham was carried north by a few escaping survivors, all reservations, all doubts, seemed to dissolve. Nottingham became the flux that welded together the North in a way that Fitzwallace, successful though he had undoubtedly been, had never quite managed to do. Nottingham, though never regarded before as anything but a town in the East Midlands, became the principal Northern rallying point. 'Remember Nottingham' people would say when doubts were thrown on the wisdom of a particular policy. 'Avenge Nottingham' became for a considerable time, almost the aim of the North's campaign.

Fitzwallace, back from his flight to meet Halford Thomas, commander of the Welsh Independence Fighters in Newport, found that Ensign Davidson, imprisoned in the Debtors' Prison in York after the St. Martin's Lane massacre, had escaped. It had been a simple, unplanned affair. Davidson, led out from the old condemned cell alone to exercise in what had been the unshackling yard, had knocked down his guard with a spanner and climbed the stone wall to freedom. The news had a depressing effect on Fitzwallace, tired after his journey and his wearying negotiations in Wales. Yet in a sense—in the context of Nottingham, in the context of the upheaval as a whole—it was an entirely trivial event. Davidson, alone, could do nothing. The prospect of his getting south through the lines was slim indeed. The chances of his early capture were very good. But Fitzwallace's reaction to the escape must be seen in perspective. He had found himself increasingly powerful. He realized that at that moment he was the only significant leader of the North. Earlier opposition to him was waning rapidly. The more tense, the more serious the situation became, the more he felt himself pushed up on to a pinnacle of isolation. The power itself he relished, but the concomitants of power—responsibility and isolation—clashed with the essential nature of his temperament. He lacked that supreme ability of delegation because he lacked the absolute conviction that there were other capable men in the world beside himself. Yet even this is not quite true: rather it was that deep inside him lay a doubt about his own ability to handle such a vast and complex situation, and this doubt he projected on to his staff. Perhaps it was not so much that he could not delegate, as that he dare not delegate. To sleep easily whilst subordinates handle complex affairs, demands a supreme self-assurance. He felt he must handle all the major complexities of the situation personally. In consequence he was tired and worn; some of the civilized panache had rubbed off him. News of Davidson's escape threw into prominence a fear he had had for some time, the fear that he was the obvious target for assassination. For without him, what leader could the North throw up at a moment's notice to replace him? He had the feeling that he was rapidly becoming irreplaceable. Totally indispensable to the Northern cause. It was a dangerous delusion and instead of taking steps to deal with the feeling itself by making the leadership as broad-based as possible, he put about himself a personal bodyguard of ten men who accompanied him everywhere. Undoubtedly this guard would have kept at arms length any potential assassin. But inevitably it also kept at arms length many of his most valuable advisers and old associates. Even Olsen found it difficult to approach him. This was particularly unfortunate. He had never seriously questioned Fitzwallace's views or actions, because he had approved so wholeheartedly of Fitzwallace himself. But now, denied his usual easy access to the singer, as it were, he began to listen more closely to the song.

Access to Rubinstein's cell was restricted to those one or two people authorized by Fitzwallace himself. Blackett was one of these. But neither Wordsworth nor Olsen had seen Rubinstein since his imprisonment. As with many organizations, however, Fitzwallace had allowed one or two of his closest associates to sign documents in his name and on his behalf. Such signatures had his formal approval. Recently he had cancelled such authorization. By a pure oversight, he had not cancelled such authorization with his wine merchant or with Pickering, the bookseller in the Shambles. Nor had he cancelled it with the guard who was responsible for Rubinstein's confinement. When Olsen, who had been responsible for sending out the cancellations on Fitzwallace's instructions, realized the omission, he signed an authorization in Fitzwallace's name for himself to visit Rubinstein. The guard on the cell door never questioned it.

The cell was dimly lit by a low-power bulb that dangled unshaded from the stone ceiling. The lighting made it appear smaller than in fact it was. The corners disappeared into dim shadows, so that they could not be defined with any accuracy. To the left of the door was a small table with an enamel washbowl and large water jug that looked as if they might have been taken straight out of an exhibition case in the Museum. Beyond the table was a wooden commode chair. The bed, an iron-framed affair of the sort that can still be seen at Army surplus sales, was placed diagonally opposite the door. Apart from the commode, the bed was the only place where a man could sit down. Rubinstein got up from it when Olsen came in. He stood very upright—almost a majestic figure, filling so much of the space of the cell. He seemed not seriously affected by the confinement. But when Olsen walked up to him he could see a tiredness behind the defiance in the eyes; a certain sagging of the flesh of his face. An aging.

'Well?' said Rubinstein. There was resignation and no friendliness in his voice.

'Can I—can I sit down?' said Olsen.

'Please,' he waved his hand towards the commode. 'That's the most comfortable place.'

Olsen sat down on the commode. He shrugged his shoulders quickly, as if trying to loosen the muscles of his back and neck.

Then he leaned forward, resting his elbows on his knees and clasping his hands. He didn't look at Rubinstein. He was wondering what exactly it was that he had come for.

'You are going to take me away?' said Rubinstein, lowering himself on to the edge of the bed.

'No,' said Olsen quickly. 'Oh, no.'

'What then?'

'I don't know. Colonel Fitzwallace might have plans—I don't know.'

Rubinstein sat quite composed on the bed and watched him staring down at the flagstone floor and working the fingers of his hands. At last he said, very quietly and gently: 'Why are you here, Sidney?'

'I don't know,' said Olsen. 'Really—I don't know.' He suddenly got up, as if he found it impossible to control the energy inside himself when he was sitting. He walked the few steps across the cell and took hold of the bars of the tiny window that looked out on to a blank stone wall beyond. 'I'm lost—you know. I'm not clear what we're doing any more—what I'm supporting. I thought you might tell me.'

'I can't tell you. We all have different visions. Unity in action is a very transitory unity. It passes with the action. It doesn't abide. For myself—I think the North has been badly treated. Our fathers put their sprawling factories over some of the most lovely and majestic countryside in Europe. All without forethought. All without any sense of the history of things. They built those square miles of slums that many of us still inhabit, buildings mean in concept and construction, buildings without dignity or aspiration, buildings founded on the view that the bulk of humanity was to be despised.'

'We've moved a little since then,' said Olsen.

'As I say,' said Rubinstein, 'it depends on the nature of one's vision. If you take the view of many Northern city Councillors that a slum is a dwelling without a lavatory and bathroom, then there has been a good deal of progress. On the other hand, if you take the view that a slum is an expression in brick of a diminished view of humanity, then it could be argued that we have slipped back. Taking the second view, you might wonder how many of our new schools and universities differ in essence from those decaying back-to-backs still to be found throughout the North. What is the soil out of which they spring? What is the view of man on which they are based? It's not a view of a creature who is fine in essence, clothed in the fineness of flesh, sensitive, innocent, good, aspiring. It's a view that says this: "Here is a head chained to a corrupt and vicious animal: how are we to contain it?" '

'But you had a vision. I knew it. I could feel it. Something—something . . .'

'Yes—something. I believe in man, the son of God. I believe in his essential goodness. I believe he is constructed for moral health. I believe him to be of all creatures the most virtuous.'

'But how can you,' cried Olsen, turning from the barred window in a burst of exasperation. 'You can see all round you evil and horror. Bloodshed outside as we talk. And you in here—what about the men who stuck you in prison?'

'I see no contradiction here. Nothing that makes me wish to change my view. When we are taught from birth to misunderstand our nature so fundamentally, how would you expect us to conduct ourselves? Church, society, education, impress on our most formative years a view of our essential rottenness; can we fully undo such conditioning in a life-time?'

'You've given your share of money to education in your time,' said Olsen irritably. He found little comfort in anything Rubinstein said. He saw a certain rosy virtue in the view he was putting forward, but could see no way of applying it to his immediate problems.

'I've made mistakes in my time,' said Rubinstein with a smile.

'What'll happen to you? What will Fitzwallace do with you?' said Olsen, sitting down again on the commode. He was tired. He thought the visit to Rubinstein had been a waste of time, a great disappointment.

'Fitzwallace? Kill me I suppose.'

'No. He wouldn't!'

'What else can he do? Be reasonable. He is totally caught up in circumstance. He must behave with consistency. Don't misunderstand me: he is a fine man. I like his vigour. I like his arrogance. But he is the product of his environment, and there is the Northern hero's tragic flaw running through him. You might live to see it overwhelm him, but I doubt I shall not.'

Olsen stared at his clenched hands. The fingers were white where he squeezed them. 'I could try to get you out,' he said at last.

'No, Sidney. What would be the point? I should have to stand up against him. There is my wife and family... No: let whatever action there is take its course. When we can sit together again like men—that will be time enough. I'm really quite comfortable here.'

'Then there's nothing I can do? Nothing?'

'Tell my wife you've seen me will you? Tell her I'm well . . .'

Olsen's increasing isolation from the leadership caused him to worry. Unless there was some sharing of power and responsibility, he felt, the Central Committee would become a farce. Sir Felix Brunton had already shown his total incompetence as a politician. There was not a trace of leadership in him. Outside the world of music, he seemed to have no interests whatever. Olsen suspected that if Brunton had been asked to state the principal aim of the Northern revolt, he would have said it was the reinstatement of Delius. Rubinstein, that well-loved patriarchal figure with his vision of a new heaven and a new earth, was now entirely out of the fight. Wordsworth alone was left, that violent, brooding country gentleman who saw the world as no more than an extension of his own estates.

Valerie Paine did not neglect to capitalise the increased intimacy between herself and Olsen that Fitzwallace was in a sense causing. It was not a conscious and calculated act on her part. There was nothing vicious in her. It was simply that, given a situation of this sort, her natural temperament could not help but take advantage of it. Her reaction was as automatic as that of one chemical juxtaposed to another with which it has a strong and God-given affinity. There was no question of any conscious decision having to be taken. Where Fitzwallace would have considered the implications of the situation in a quite cool and deliberate way, she operated like a reflex muscle action where the conscious areas of the mind, and those debilitating moral considerations associated with it, were by-passed.

'Look at you, Sidney,' she said as she lay beside him. 'You can't go on like this. Have you seen yourself in the mirror? Those puffy eyes, these lines above your nose.' She put her fingertips on his brow and tried to smooth away the lines. 'You must give yourself a chance. You must relax.'

'What was he like when you knew him?' said Olsen, taking her hand in his and kissing the tips of her fingers.

'Fitzwallace? Oh, he was a man,' she said. She could see him in the eyes of her memory with his easy charm, his smile, the glittering monocle with which he made such dramatic play. 'He must have been very frightening to some people. His manner could change in a second. He could be so icy. But he never frightened me.'

'No one could frighten you,' he said with a smile.

'You frighten me now.'

'You're teasing.'

'You frighten me because if you go on working and worrying like this, you'll kill yourself. No one can stand it. And what are you? You're no more than a boy, with these sad brown eyes of yours and this mop of hair. You're made for better things than war. Think of all the pleasure you've given the world with this pop culture of yours. You've really made people feel good. That's more than most people ever do. It's more than I've ever done.'

'Not you,' he said. 'You've made me feel good. You've made me feel warm and alive.'

'This is better isn't it—lying here feeling warm and alive—than all this playing at soldiers?'

He propped himself up on an elbow and said: 'You don't know the North, do you? What do you know about us really? You used to come here during August for the grouse shooting. That isn't the North. The North's bare and sad. It's wild. It doesn't give a damn about people. Savage, you know, at times. The excitement of all that power lying just under the surface. Have you never felt it? It lies like an animal ready to strike. Here you are thinking about it as if it were a little private zoo full of brown birds for you to shoot at.'

'You could show me,' she said. 'You could explain. I want to know. No one's ever bothered to explain you and your country.'

'Our country,' he said. 'Yes it is. And why the hell should we explain it—to you or to anyone else? Why? Do you go around explaining London? No. If people want to know about it you leave them to find out. Well why don't you take the trouble to find out? Why don't you get out of your cars and look at it? Go to Northumberland—Otterburn, Alnwick. Go up the Tees from Piercebridge beyond High Force. Go to Haworth in December . . .'

She laughed. 'My goodness,' she said. 'What a lather you're in.'

'Oh,' he said. 'You take nothing seriously. Why do I bother?'

'I take you very seriously,' she said, laying a hand on his bare shoulder. 'But how can I go in any case? The road-blocks, the guards at every corner. And I'm virtually a prisoner too, whatever you say.'

'No,' he said, 'I suppose you can't.'

'Of course,' she said softly. 'You could take me. With you there'd be no problems of movement.'

'No, it's out of the question. Impossible. Really—at a time like this.'

'For me? For my sake?'

'No. Not for you.'

'Then for heaven's sake for yourself. Can't you see you can't go on like this, driving yourself for nothing. And be realistic for one moment—are you really so utterly indispensable, just for a few hours? Let's get away for just one day. Who would miss you for just one day? The "cause"—is that it? Darling, the cause is launched. It'll run itself now to the bitter end, whatever anyone does. Later, you might be able to help it again—control it perhaps. Not now. Not in this state.'

'God I am so tired. Do you tire me—is that it?'

'No,' she said. 'I don't tire you. But you tire yourself for nothing. Rest for a day. Get away from here for one day. Show me this North you talk about.'

'Well—' he said, considering whether it would be possible.

'Tomorrow. Say you'll take me tomorrow.'

'Well I'll see,' he said, getting up.

Next morning, over breakfast, he said: 'Well all right. I've got hold of a Landrover. It's against my better judgement, but all right.'

He worked for an hour, sorting papers and giving instructions into the tape-recorder. He tried to see Fitzwallace, but failed. Fitzwallace was engaged, he was told, with Dr. Blackett. Blackett had moved in the past few days closer and closer to the centre of power.

Valerie put an arm through his as they walked down the stone steps to the vehicle. 'You'll be glad, you know,' she said. 'Glad I pulled you out.' She was bright with a little sense of achievement at having persuaded him to break his routine.

They drove down Bootham where troops were billeted in the Quaker School, and out through the Clifton roadblock where a tall young lieutenant threw up a brisk salute and three soldiers came quickly to attention when they saw the pennant on the wing of the car. Then through Skelton, where the full-leaved sycamores and chestnuts bowed across the road, and down the bleak mainstreet of Shipton.

'Where are we going?' she said at last, looking at his silent profile still with the drawn lines deep above the nose. A handsome, a good-looking boy, she thought, with that open face and dark hair. She wondered what she thought of him—really. If she thought anything. For that matter, did she think anything of anybody? Fitzwallace? Not any more certainly. And Robert? Well, Robert—she refused to believe that she'd ever really let him down. Looked at in one way, she'd never even been unfaithful to him, if infidelity meant a total giving of oneself to someone else. That, she thought, a little sadly, she'd never really done. Perhaps, just for a moment to Robert, in the very early days. But she'd snatched that final last little core of herself back quickly enough. There was something of a game about it all. A feeling that if you were ever seriously challenged on it, you could always withdraw. You could always say you weren't really serious. Which meant you never could be really serious. She put the considerations out of her head with a practised mental shrug.

'Well, this is due north,' said Olsen. 'The old coaching road through Northallerton. Don't judge us by this. This isn't very exciting.'

But it was warm and fresh. The air was fresh and clean after the stuffiness of York. So humid really, and even with the windows wide open no air seemed to move through them. Rather like those dour Ibsen plays, throught Valerie, about dead people in airless rooms, and the death of the heart.

'Exciting or not,' she laughed, 'what a change!'

'Can't you see them clattering up here with that coach and six, with their coats open in the hot afternoons? More likely buttoned up against the rain though. What a sight that must have been!'

'What before that?' she said.

'Before the coaches? Horses, I suppose. And before that the Vikings coming in from the sea. Pillaging, raping, burning, carrying off into slavery—all that sort of romantic stuff. Then before that the Romans: a cold and docile lot, you know. Straight roads plodding straight through the woods and swamps, up the hills and down the valleys. On and on and on. They'd no feel for anything those stiff little Italians.'

'You do hate outsiders,' she said.

'Well perhaps,' he said. 'No it's not that really; not outsiders. You're an outsider; I don't hate you. But anyone hates exploiters. We feel we've been exploited—always. We feel the cream of the country, its wealth, its energy, have all been drained away into the South. Someone in the past took the plug out of the bath. We've never managed to get it back.'

The road ran down the centre of the broad valley. On either side, in the distance, hills rolled upwards, with little farms perched among them. There were stretches of unbroken woodland, dark green in the distance. They turned along the valley of the Tees, west towards its source. There the woods were deep and lush. Oak, sycamore and ash, spreading long branches over the shallow water. A man stood amongst the stones in the middle of the river, fishing a deep and shaded pool. The river chattered over the stones, or sank into the blackness under the tree branches.

They had lunch in the *Rose and Crown* in Romaldkirk and then crossed the river into Durham. The climb from the river into Egglestone was so deeply wooded that only the smallest amount of light filtered through on to the road. On the right, below the road, a stream toppled quickly down to the river, dropping over rocks, bubbling over the thick and mossy roots of trees. Then suddenly they were in the full clear sunlight again, and ahead rose the moors touched with blue in the distance. They climbed up to the ridge above the valley. There, standing at the roadside, leaning over a black stone wall, they could see the whole panoramic display of South Durham and north Yorkshire, rolling away towards the west into Lancashire, Cumberland and Westmorland. The distance was blue running into purple. Whitewashed farmhouses and farm buildings, widely separated, stood out from the few points of shelter in the landscape. A mile away, below them in the valley bottom, ran the broad river deep in the shadow of the trees.

'Come on,' he said, running the vehicle into a wood of larch and spruce, 'let's climb up there.'

Higher, even the scrubby grass at which a few sinewy sheep were nibbling, grew barer. Stretches of bare black rock appeared. Ahead, columns of rock rose up from the moor, breaking up into the sky from the undulating horizon. Amongst the gigantic stones, they lay in a gentle depression covered by short moss-filled grass, and looked down over the vast landscape that rolled and tumbled into the far west. The sun was hot above them, and the sky was bright with light. In the far blue distance, the horizon met the sky in an indeterminate haze.

'There you are,' he said, as if it were all his.

'You sound a bit like God,' she laughed. 'As if you'd created it all and were pleased.'

'Well—perhaps,' he said.

'It's beautiful,' she said. 'I agree, it is beautiful.' But even on this day of high summer, she felt a wind touching her face with icy fingers. She felt that the land could be warmed and wooed by the sun only so far. Always at the back there was this shadow of winter.

She let him undress her. She watched with amusement as he placed her clothes carefully and one by one in a little pile on the edge of the depression. Lying there naked under the hot sun, she felt really that only sensuality mattered. Not wars and politics and silly affairs of the head. What was the head after all, but a chunk of corruption stuck on top of a healthy animal? She had been through the business of physical love so many times, and it never palled. He kissed her lips and ears, her throat and shoulders, and she lay there smiling at him and doing nothing. He looked so young and vigorous, with his broad shoulders and firm flesh and dark hair brushing against her. The wrinkles above his nose had quite gone. He kissed her breasts and lifted the nipples with the tips of his fingers. He kissed the smooth, warm mound of her abdomen. He kissed her thighs, and at last she put out her arms and drew him on top of her, and when the climax came and they lay convulsed together, inextricably entwined, like some single new form of animal, she thought: 'Damn if I have a child, does it matter?' But as he lay there still entwined with her, not moving now, she looked past his bare shoulder into the bright sky, and there was still this part of her that kept itself to itself. A part that refused to give up its identity. Why should she want to? Why should she want just for once to have every part of her consciousness obliterated? She thought to herself: I think I'm not capable of loving anyone. The thought left her with a bitter sense of unsatisfactoriness.

'Hm?' muttered Olsen, lifting his head a little.

'Nothing,' she said. 'I didn't say anything.'

'I love you,' he muttered.

She thought: What a shame for you.

The Southern 1st Army, under the command of General Sir Maxwell Howard, advanced jubilantly from Nottingham. But resistance, instead of being broken as Howard had expected, merely stiffened the further north he went. Pushing through the Dukeries with the intention of breaking the Northern line between Worksop and Retford, he found Sherwood Forest full of opposing troops. They were well dug-in and supplied, and they knew the country from personal acquaintance with it. Moreover, it was their country, not Howard's. The men of Nottinghamshire were fighting for their own property, whilst the Southerners were not. Much of the fighting was hand-to-hand and bloody. It was not sufficient for Howard to put himself in a superior tactical position and expect the opposition to surrender. None surrendered. To occupy a machinegun or mortar position, meant having to kill every single man in that position. Finally, a mile south of A620, Howard's principal drive came to a halt by mid-June. He began to dig in.

News of Howard's failure to make the expected progress, brought pressure on the PM from a number of civilian as well as military quarters to use nuclear weapons. Strong arguments were put forward, principally on the grounds of saving life, for subjecting five Northern cities to limited nuclear attack. The argument that part of the country's nuclear armament was in fact in the North and could presumably be used in reprisal, was countered by the conviction that if the initial attacks were carried out with sufficient determination, reprisals of any kind would no longer be possible. It was the City of London that tipped the balance against nuclear attack on the North, by throwing its enormous weight behind the PM. Sir Clupton Everarrd stated the City's case: 'The destruction of the means of production of the North, together with any considerable reduction in Northern purchasing power, could prove a most serious embarrassment to the City's investments in that area.'

During the early hours of June 27th, the Northern counter-offensive began. The main Southern thrust had been towards the North-east, with the aim of occupying the industrial centres of the West Riding and the City of York itself, before driving through Darlington to Tyneside. In consequence, General Sir Wilson Smith's 1st Northern Army found only light, sporadic opposition to its movement south from the Lancashire border. Wilson Smith's aim was to turn the left flank of the Southern army, and then break through to the east at a point south of Leek.

Howard, commanding the Southern thrust to the North-east, had completely misjudged the outcome of the Nottingham bombardment. A man without any sensitivity to human psychology, he still imagined that Nottingham had been the death blow to the Northern revolt. The opposition he was meeting, though stiff and even fanatical in places, he saw as the last death throes of a dying animal. He firmly believed, against all reports and rumours to the contrary, that a collapse was inevitable. And that collapse he expected at any moment.

This supreme self-confidence of an essentially stupid man, was Wilson Smith's principal ally. He passed quickly over bridges that should have been destroyed; his supply convoys ran easily down roads that should have been mined. Only from the air did he meet with any serious opposition, and against this he had the support of his own substantial air cover. He realized how successfully his own part of the counter-offensive was developing, when, moving down M6 towards Brickhouses, he passed groups of his own paratroopers who had been dropped during the night. They had their helmets off. They were smoking and leaning over the parapets of the bridges they had been sent to defend. They had met no serious opposition of any kind. The bridges had not even been prepared for demolition by the retreating Southern forces. By the end of the day, his forward patrols were moving east from Ashbourne.

At dawn, Vultures of the Northern 24 Group had attacked troop concentrations and concentrations of armour and supplies from Chesterfield to Lincoln. Howard's forward headquarters outside Gamston had been badly hit. General Lionel Quigley's Northern 3rd Army had been moving into positions along the south bank of the Humber for days. In the first glimmering of light they began to move south. They met fierce and well-organized resistance along the line of the Scunthorpe-Grimsby road, but shortly before midday they had broken through the Southern line between Brigg and Melton Ross and begun pouring through the breech. East of the breech, there was nothing for the Southerners to do but withdraw to avoid encirclement and possible decimation. By early evening, Quigley himself ran up the Northern flag in Lincoln.

But to view the developing situation in terms of clear-cut front lines, moving in classical manner back and forth, would be to over-simplify to the point of complete inaccuracy. News of the counter-attack roused local groups within the area occupied by Southern troops, to firm and immediate resistance. Nottingham had done far more than inflame the North. It had inflamed people everywhere against an act of ruthless oppression by a central authority. A corps commander passing through Market Rasen was disemboweled by a publican whose parents had burnt to death in Nottingham. In a ditch by the side of the Newark by-pass, three medical orderlies moving up to the front in an ambulance, were soaked in petrol and set on fire by a group of sixth formers from the new Comprehensive at Coddington. In a number of places, patrols were ambushed and totally destroyed, by organized resistance fighters. Even as far to the south of the main fighting area as Kettering, an ammunition supply convoy of four lorries was blown up on the southern approach to the town. A plague of minor setbacks hit the Southern troops, from the discovery of water and sand in petrol tanks to slashed tyres, smashed distributor heads and bricks thrown through windscreens. To the commanders, the line might have been represented on a map by an organized movement of little flags. But in fact, the fighting, both major and minor, went on for a depth of thirty or forty miles. Accurate information was hard to come by. Rumours sprang up and spread.

The next day, General Howard was in a deep bunker a mile south-east of his old headquarters. A continuous artillery barrage was slamming down to his right along the line of the Retford-Gainsborough road. He had lost all contact with London. His information on the total situation was hours behind the real facts. Even his picture of the situation in the Worksop Bulge, as it was becoming known, was sketchy in the extreme. He still believed that he was facing a strong, but limited action, restricted to his own immediate front. Rumours that Lincoln had fallen the night before, he continuously refused to believe. By mid-afternoon, all his contact with the outside world had gone. He was isolated in the northern section of the bulge by Northern troops in front and on both flanks, and by the Nottinghamshire Resistance to his rear. Fortunately for the Southern 1st Army, the points of the Northern pincers closing on Hucknall from Belper in the west and Newark in the east, were slowed sufficiently by the brilliant resistance organized by Brigadier Anderson, to allow the vast majority of Southern forces to be withdrawn. The trap closed finally in the late morning of the next day. Quigley and Wilson Smith met and shook hands with obvious satisfaction. It was now just a question of mopping up the remnants of the Southern 1st Army still inside the trap.

At such a time, the question of communication becomes vital. Howard, issuing orders from his forward bunker, was self-absorbed and unimaginative. But he was not an utter fool in military matters. If he had known the seriousness of the threat to his rear, he would have withdrawn. The fact is that he simply did not know. He had been brought up in his military youth on tales of disaster in the First World War arising from attempts to command from a distance. From the days of his first action, it had been his boast: 'Where the bullets are, I am.' But he made the mistake of all unimaginative men. He believed he had discovered a principle of command applicable to all situations for all time.

His first realization of his lack of touch with the real situation came with the sound of heavy gun-fire immediately to his south, during the morning of June 29th. There was no way in which he could account for it. None of his own artillery positions was so far behind and so exactly south of him. He was aware of sporadic attacks within his lines, by resistance fighters, but it would have been impossible for them to bring artillery to bear in any numbers. He sent out a patrol, only to learn the alarming news that a concentration of Anderson's men was being attacked by artillery of the Northern 1st Army. Further patrols confirmed the news and established that Howard was isolated in an area of some forty square miles. 'No,' he said. 'No. I can't believe it. They can't have moved so quickly. They can't have made such a breakthrough. Impossible.' He pored over the map again, stubbing his finger at the points where he knew for certain the enemy had been. But the evidence against his disbelief was overwhelming: the total absence of any Southern support aircraft, the heavy gunfire in his rear, the reports of his patrols. The resilience that experience had instilled in him, finally took over. Despite what he regarded as his better judgement he decided to accept the facts and act in the light of them. He began to reorganize the forces within his isolated box. He planned to make an attempt to break out to the south.

But when he began to move, it was obvious at once that the route to the south was totally closed. The pincers had taken a firm grip north of Nottingham, and were beginning to tighten further. The picked and hardened men of the Northern 1st and 3rd Armies were in that direction. He had no hope of breaking through them. To the north, the enemy was still opposing him in force along the Worksop-Retford road. If they had once brought to a standstill his entire advance, there was little chance of breaking through them with his vastly diminished force. Which left him a simple choice between the east and the west. And really even there there was no proper choice. To the east there were the flat lands towards the Lincolnshire border, with little cover from either the ground or the air. To the west, at least there were the remaining woods of Sherwood Forest, and beyond them the rolling Pennine foothills. That way there might be a chance. He concentrated his forces for a push to the west, intending, when the pressure eased, to wheel to the south.

He broke through the lines of Wilson Smith's 1st Army late in the evening, after savage local encounters on a very restricted front. Once through, it was not difficult to pass quickly to the west. For one thing, the breakout was so unexpected, that news of it took some time to reach Wilson Smith, now established outside Hucknall. It took longer for the news to be confirmed to Wilson Smith's satisfaction. For another thing, the uniforms and equipment of both sides were identical, so that it was possible to move a quite large body of men and machines through the forward areas without challenge. But when he reached Staveley, on the Worksop-Chesterfield road, and tried to wheel south, he met immediate and heavy resistance. Word of the break-out had clearly reached 1st Army headquarters. Any real stand was now out of the question, since the element of surprise had gone. They were being driven by increasing pressure from the south to swing further to the north. When daylight came, a large body of men and equipment would be a sitting target for the fighter-bombers. He was left with no alternative but to split his force into small units, in the hope that each would stand a better chance of avoiding detection. Where direct confrontation of the enemy would now be suicidal, stealth and guile might conceivably succeed.

Howard himself retained a body of two hundred men and

such light equipment as they could carry. He left his transport and took to the open country. He hoped that by morning, he might be in the higher more isolated reaches of the Derbyshire Pennines. There it might be possible to find concealment from the helicopters he knew would be looking for him. But it meant a march across strange country, and across the trunk road from Sheffield to the South, a march of some fifteen or twenty miles, and even then he had calculated too optimistically. At times the march became a running battle in the darkness, with patrols of the 1st Army on the look-out for them, dazzling them with portable searchlights through the woods. And despite the darkness, helicopters clattered continuously in the vicinity, dropping brilliant flares from time to time, that hung in the air minutes on end, lighting up the entire landscape. They had to cross the Sheffield-Chesterfield road in little groups of three or four, waiting for a gap in the patrolling vehicles, waiting for the low-flying helicopters to move away north or south, then running with a sudden clatter of boots across the tarmac surface and dropping into the ditch on the far side.

Towards Holmesfield, they ran into a group of resistance fighters. There were no more than twenty of them, but they knew every piece of cover in the area. Darkness seemed scarcely any hindrance to them. Howard's men were caught in a hail of machinegun fire and light mortar bombs. The encounter was brief. The resistance men, vastly outnumbered, withdrew after their advantage of surprise had gone. But in that first violent burst of fire, Howard had suffered thirty-two casualties. The dead and wounded had to be left, in the hope that they would be picked up shortly by the enemy and given whatever attention was necessary. And certainly they were given attention, for the group of resistance fighters, following Howard's trail now from a distance, came across them groaning and crying out in the night. They left not one alive. They stripped them of their uniforms, equipment and personal belongings. The body of Lieutenant Fordyce, who had listened to Howard's philosophy of war during the Nottingham bombardment, they strung up by one foot from a tree. 'He'll show us which way the wind blows,' said one of them.

Throughout the night harrying and sniping went on. There was no major encounter, but innumerable minor running engagements cost Howard many men. A few deserted to the North. Some tried to give themselves up and were shot. Others, straggling behind the main body because of wounds, were shot by the prowling resistance fighters. When the first light of day appeared, just bringing into definition the horizon in Howard's rear, the resistance fighters were still in contact with him. In fifteen minutes the day would bring the fighter bombers. His immediate force had dwindled during the night to less than fifty men. Movement during the day would be out of the question. He looked around for cover. Ahead, some three or four hundred yards, an outcrop of rock swelled above the level of the surrounding land. There, amongst the black boulders and deep cleft rocks, he made preparations to defend himself until darkness fell again. He saw the resistance fighters in the distance. Some of them were women. They marked where he had drawn up, and then sat down to wait for instructions.

News of the fact that this group of Southerners was commanded by Howard, the 'Butcher of Nottingham' as he was now widely known, was given by a deserter to a resistance commander. It reached General Wilson Smith in the early morning. Major Ramsden was given the responsibility of capturing Howard alive. It was for this reason that Howard's group had got so far. Ramsden had issued instructions to the resistance, not to close decisively with the group in case Howard himself was killed in the fighting. Ramsden arrived with a company of men before Howard's position a little after 5 in the morning. The day was bright. The mass of rocks stood up black above the skyline. Through binoculars he could see Howard's men looking down towards him over the open ground between them. He thought it would not be easy to prise them out and take Howard alive. He moved forward under cover of light armour and dropped tear gas bombs into Howard's position. The gas brought many of the defenders out into the open, their eyes red and weeping, their hands raised high in the air. The resistance fighters shot them as they appeared, despite Ramsden's orders. It complicated the situation further, for it meant that the remaining defenders chose to stay under cover, burying their faces in handkerchiefs and battledress blouses until the light wind had cleared the air of gas. The last hard core of under twenty men, had to be driven out at bayonet point. But the hardest job facing Ramsden that morning, was to keep the resistance men away from Howard. Given the chance, they would have torn him to pieces there and then. But Ramsden got him into one of the armoured vehicles, and at General Wilson Smith's headquarters it was decided to send him under heavy guard to York.

If Howard had returned to London, he would unquestionably have been cashiered. The official attitude to the Nottingham bombardment was that it was an act far beyond Howard's brief. Certainly it had hardened, rather than softened or crushed, resistance. The PM himself regarded it as an act of such breathtaking stupidity, as to be almost incredible. Paine felt deeply sickened by the news. He saw the bombardment as an act that made the slim possibility of negotiation now totally impossible. He saw, stretching before them, weeks—perhaps months—of bloody and bitter fighting. In his more pessimistic moments, when he was particularly tired and his leg gave him trouble, he could not imagine a time in the future when the deep wound inflicted by Howard would ever have healed. It would leave a bitterness running through three or four generations.

Yet there were those who, unofficially, were elated by the news from Nottingham. This, they felt, was the kind of ruthless stand that should be taken against the insurrectionists. Sir Clapham Tinkler was particularly outspoken. In the board room of the Northern Shipping Society's offices in Holborn, he said: 'Force is the only argument these peasants understand. What the devil is there up there worth fighting for? Filth and smoke and rain. This quality of life they talk about; what's it amount to? Drink and fornication! That's life for these Northerners—drink and fornication. I shan't be satisfied until I see a dozen Nottinghams throughout that blighted country-side, and a million barbarians roasting in the ashes.'

Tinkler, and dozens of influential men, lobbied Parliament continuously, demanding the most savage prosecution of the war. The PM could sidestep some of this pressure, and with-stand a good deal of the rest. But inevitably it had some effect.

146

As the Northern counter-offensive gathered momentum, Paine was negotiating with foreign governments for the cutting off of supplies to the Northern ports. In New York, the government put its case to the United Nations, and pleaded for a total embargo on all supplies being sent to the rebels.

The church made constant pleas for peace. When Fitzwallace read a report of a statement by the Archbishop of Canterbury, he snapped: 'Let them look to Jerusalem. The centre of our world is half-way between Newcastle and Oslo, at the bottom of the North Sea.' And Fitzwallace could make such Olympian pronouncements, for as he spoke the Northern armies continued to push steadily south.

Dr. Sidney Blackett had by now almost replaced Olsen in the tiny circle of Fitzwallace's confidence. Blackett had those faculties that Fitzwallace required at that stage. Shrewd, authoritative, powerful, he made an admirable aide. True, he still had no place on the Central Committee, but the Council of the North was so completely dominated by Fitz-wallace that the Committee ceased to do more than give formal support to everything he did. Wordsworth, bitter and scheming, gave his formal support to Fitzwallace's activities, because no other course was open to him. But he was playing constantly upon Jackman's opposition to Fitzwallace.

Olsen began to feel himself redundant. The work he now did seemed increasingly less important, less concerned with the real centre of the revolution. In the early days of the rising, his idealism and enthusiasm had helped him to give himself completely to work that he was not temperamentally suited to. But now, increasingly isolated from the mainspring of power, suffering increasingly from a sense of guilt at the horrors that he had helped to unleash, he became dispirited and dis-illusioned. He was surprised one morning to find two guards waiting outside his office, with instructions to take him to Fitzwallace. Inside, Fitzwallace was pacing back and forth. Two further guards stood by the window, sub-machine guns in their hands. Blackett was seated in a heavy leather chair by the table, nodding gently as Fitzwallace spoke. Olsen stood inside the door for a moment. At last he spoke, and Fitzwallace turned to him.

'Ah, Sidney,' said Fitzwallace. He seemed to be his old self. He smiled and walked over to Olsen and shook his hand warmly. 'I don't see nearly enough of you these days, Sidney. Pressing affairs of state, you know.' He gave a little laugh and waved Olsen to a chair. He turned back to Blackett and continued talking. Blackett watched him as he walked first to the window and then back to the table. Blackett sat with his shoulders hunched, his eyes taking in Fitzwallace's every movement. Something was seriously changed about Fitzwallace, Olsen thought, that he should have taken such a man into his confidence. A man with such ambition burning in his eyes. To Olsen, there seemed to be something unbelievably cunning in Blackett. He was not so much listening to Fitzwallace, as studying him. It reminded him of those stories he had heard of American political circles, where a man studies film of his opponent in the hope of detecting his weak points, where he seeks to identify himself with his opponent and experience his mental processes with the intention of seeing how those processes might be upset. Even now, isolated in his rooms, protected by his bodyguard, Fitzwallace seemed very vulnerable.

Back at the table, Fitzwallace pointed with his swordstick to points on a relief map of the country that had been assembled. 'It's a question of controlling them,' he was saying. 'The vigour, the energy—you need to experience it. *Dinas Vawr*—you know the poem? They'll sweep across the South-west like demons when Halford Thomas blows his bugle.'

'We don't mind that, do we?' said Blackett.

'We may do,' said Fitzwallace, after considering the question for a moment. 'Will they stop when they reach our armies? The point is the old one, you see—what is the North and what is the South? Who are we fighting and who are they fighting? We've seen that the old definition doesn't apply. The North doesn't finish at Bawtry as we used to believe. The North finishes wherever we run into opposition. Nottingham was our greatest ally, and we didn't realise it. Lincoln didn't oppose us. Now the Welsh are marching. They tell me they're marching shoulder to shoulder with us against the South. I think they're really marching by themselves against the English. Who can blame them? But they could mistake us for Englishmen before they notice we're Northerners. I've stressed this to Halford Thomas, but I question the control he has over his men when they smell blood. Get in touch with Wilson Smith. Make quite sure he knows what to be on the lookout for. Tell him I've delayed them as long as I can. They're moving east at midnight.'

Blackett left the room, with his brisk, determined walk. He seemed always to have clearly in his mind only one immediate goal at a time. Fitzwallace sat in the leather chair Blackett had just vacated, and dropped his head into his hands. He seemed tired in every fibre of his body. At last he seemed to remember Olsen. He lifted his head, adjusted his monocle and smiled.

'Then the Welsh are marching?' said Olsen.

'Hm? Yes, Sidney. The Welsh are marching. There'll be some blood spilt.' He sounded as if the idea was distasteful to him.

'It's difficult to see you these days,' said Olsen.

Fitzwallace nodded. 'I intend it to be, Sidney.'

'We began with a democratic movement for liberation,' said Olsen.

'So we did,' said Fitzwallace. 'A fine, peacetime ideal. Bear it in mind for the future, Sidney. A comfortable, distant star to contemplate from a deck chair in an apple orchard.'

'What's happened to you?' said Olsen.

'Perhaps I'm getting old. Victory—that's what I'm concerned with at the moment. Just damn' well winning. What's that they say? "Win the war, the peace will take care of itself." '

'I've never heard that.'

'Perhaps I said it.'

'Well it seems that the war's being won. Isn't it time to think about the peace. You must have some ideas—some plans. What's to happen when we've won? How are we to govern? I saw a new society, a new kind of life growing up, a richness. I saw a splendid race of new men emerging . . .'

'I know you did. You were always one for the broad vision, Sidney. No doubt there'll be a place for your kind somewhere in the future. But not now; not in the present.'

'This is why you called me in?'

'Yes,' Fitzwallace sat for a moment. Then he got up quickly and snapped: 'Look, it's not easy. I never saw myself in this position when we started. Believe it or not—it's immaterial to me. What am I? An adventurer, I suppose. Nothing more, really. But one man doesn't control a situation like this. I didn't get here by a deliberate act of choice, and then a climb up on my own shoelaces. You and Wordsworth and a million others pushed me forward. But I'm here, and we can't change it . . . I'm telling you this, because I want you to know how much you're responsible for what's happened. Your enthusiasm, you idealism—things would have been different without them. But I can't use them any more. This isn't the time for such things.'

'But good God!' said Olsen, getting up and pacing round the table. 'If this isn't the time for some statement of ideals and principles, when is? What would you have me do—let the whole movement blunder on into darkness? Look, see me like this: see me as a gadfly that reminds you of the larger issues. See me as a questioner of actions. See me as a conscience that can be overruled, but not ignored . . .'

'You tire me Sidney.' He was standing at the window, looking out over the courtyard and the lawns. A guard was being changed outside the old Castle Museum. The shouts of the guard-commander rang out over the quiet summer air. High over the bare walls of Clifford's Tower, a formation of bombers drummed towards the south. 'I'm relieving you of your duties. Blackett's taking over from you.'

'Blackett?'

'Yes Blackett. I don't want your comments. Just carry out my instructions. Perhaps when it's over . . . I'm not having you confined. You're not a prisoner in any way. You can stay in your rooms here if you wish, or you can move away. But you're not one of us any more. There's no place for you here. This isn't a time for asking questions. And Mrs. Paine—you'd better make whatever arrangements for her that you want. I leave her to you. But let me tell you this: she's not for you. Get rid of her before she poisons you.'

Wordsworth's seeds took some time to germinate in Jackman's mind. Jackman was a man who needed always to clarify a decision intellectually, before acting on it. He seemed to feel that to have the motive for a projected action clearly in his consciousness, gave that action an unchallengeable 'rightness'. When he had thrashed out the intellectual implications of action, that action became just. Justice was intellectual acceptability. This process cost him much energy and moral soul-searching. He found it difficult to sleep at night, as the problem bore upon him. He lay on his back staring at the bedroom ceiling, turning over one point again and again. He was an example of that infinite capacity for taking pains, which certainly has nothing to do with genius. During lectures to his students, he found his inner preoccupation with Fitzwallace's dictatorial behaviour actually coming to the surface, so that whole phrases, erupting from this deeper process, were injected into his pronouncements on Euripidean tragedy. His students, with whom he had always been a popular if slightly remote man began to wonder what was happening to him. He suffered all the anguish of a deep moral conflict, intellectualized to the point where its resolution in action had become impossible. It was at this point that Wordsworth forced his hand.

Fitzwallace was due to give a progress report to the full Council of the North the next morning. He arrived, as Wordsworth had expected, a little late and attended by six of his personal guard, whom he insisted stayed in the Council Chamber during the meeting. As far as Fitzwallace was concerned he intended nothing arrogant by the move. He was convinced that he had reached the point where threats to his life were a real possibility. As it turned out, his judgement was right. But to the members of the Council, increasingly in the dark as to what the real situation was, and what Fitzwallace intended as his next move in their name, it rang out as a challenge to the Council itself. Wordsworth did his best as chairman, to encourage these feelings to develop. To Jackman, Fitzwallace seemed to be the archetype of dictatorial arrogance from the beginning of history. Wordsworth, watching him whenever the opportunity allowed, could almost see the moment when he reached his decision. Wordsworth, at the same moment, made the decision not to let Jackman out of his sight until the thing was done.

The problem was to get Jackman close enough to Fitzwallace. He was quite inaccessible in his headquarters in the Debtors' Prison, surrounded by his bodyguard. It would have to be done outside. Perhaps on one of Fitzwallace's journeys. Perhaps at some meeting. The weapon would be a pistol.

The next morning, the Welsh, under the leadership of Halford Thomas, marched to the east on a front extending from Newport to Abergavenny. It was not until they reached positions east of Gloucester, that Fitzwallace's doubts about their discipline began to be justified. The air was full of Welsh songs as they passed through Cheltenham and Cirencester. The deeper they drove unopposed into England, the more enthusiastic and excited they became. They smashed shop windows in Fairford, and when the southern spearhead reached Swindon they began, without any apparent provocation from the inhabitants, to sack and burn the town. From the Cotswolds to Southampton, people left their homes before the advancing Welsh forces, and moved east and south. They crammed the roads with cars, full of sad-eyed, frightened children. They moved in hired lorries, loaded with all their movable goods—beds and bedding, television sets protected by mattresses, precious pieces of newly-acquired furniture. They formed miles of solid jams along the road to Reading. All traffic in Winchester came to a standstill. Southern troops pushed them off M4 with bulldozers and tanks, to keep the road open for the defending army to advance. But still they came, with the clamour of the victorious Welsh at their heels. And wherever they passed, the invaders left a trail of pillage and destruction. Women were raped, men burnt to death. Advance patrol aircraft, supporting Wilson Smith's 1st Army, continuing to move south from the North-west, reported a pall of smoke moving from the west towards London.

9

Howard lay imprisoned for a week, isolated from the other prisoners in a tiny cell in the Debtors' Prison. The door was of six inch timber, reinforced with strips of iron riveted through. There was a grille in the door that opened from time to time, so that a guard could inspect the prisoner. When it opened, a little extra light filtered into the gloomy cell from the corridor outside. The only permanent source of light and air, was a hole high in the wall measuring no more than six inches square and covered by two thick round bars of iron. On the stone walls themselves, were the carvings of earlier prisoners: 'Sentenced 7 yeres stransported', one of them read. It was dated March 2nd, 1819.

For three days Fitzwallace had succeeded in keeping the whereabouts of Howard a secret. But it was inevitable that the secret would leak out. A guard talked to his wife about the prisoner. A woman cleaner heard an officer mention Howard's name as she worked in the corridor outside Fitzwallace's apartments. There was speculation in the town at first, as the rumours began to run through the pubs and cafés. Could it really be that the Debtors' Prison here in York, actually held that notorious killer? The rumours took new and alarming turns every hour. There was a plot to send a commando force from the South to release Howard. There was a plot from within the North to spirit him away through a secret underground passage to the river. From there by water to Hull and from Hull to London. Forty-eight hours, they said, was all it would take to put Howard back behind his murderous forces. And then what would happen? His capture and imprisonment could hardly be expected to have softened his attitude to the North. Demonstrations took place as near to Fitzwallace's headquarters as the guards would allow. They demanded Howard's immediate execution. And as the days passed, the demonstrations became more frequent and more vociferous. Men and women who had somehow escaped from Nottingham, spoke to the demonstrators. They showed wounds and burns, still not completely healed. They talked of unimaginable horrors. They filled the crowds with fear and horror. Above all they filled them with revenge. Under this mounting pressure, Fitzwallace at last ordered that Howard be brought to trial.

Everyone regarded the trial as a farce. Nottingham would lie in ruins for a generation. Here was the man responsible. What was there to try? If he were found guilty, then a trial would have been a costly and time-wasting way of reaching the conclusion that the town had already reached. If he were found innocent, then was it conceivable that he would be allowed to live?

The rear committee room on the first floor of Fitzwallace's headquarters, had been turned into a court-room. Its windows looked out on to the high stone wall at the back of the building. It was the same wall that Olsen had stared at when he was working in his room along the corridor. A large, baize-covered table stood in the middle of the room, directly under a vast chandelier of sparkling crystal. Three doors opened into the room; one from the corridor outside, the other two from a small adjoining room. A dock had been erected in front of the table, and to one side. Facing the dock were two rows of leather chairs, placed for the Committee of Judgement which had been selected from the Council of the North. Wordsworth, as chairman of the Council, had been careful to select Jackman as a member of the Committee of Judgement, though the President of the Committee itself was of course Fitzwallace.

The indictment was made and witnesses gave evidence throughout the morning. Blackett sat on Fitzwallace's right, watching the witnesses, watching Howard and making notes. Fitzwallace turned to him from time to time as if asking his advice. A kind of *eminence grise*, thought Jackman. A woman from Sherwood described the aerial bombardment in vivid and painful detail. She had lost her husband and three sons in the fires. A captain from General Quigley's command, talked about the horror and destruction he found when he marched into the ruined city. A boy was wheeled in in an invalid chair, but broke down during the questioning. Jackman was outraged by what he heard. It hardened still further his feelings against Fitzwallace, whom he saw as the first cause of it all. He saw himself increasingly as an instrument of justice. His mind became obsessed with one single purpose. From time to time he slipped his hand into his jacket pocket. Wordsworth, watching him with growing satisfaction, knew he had his hand on the revolver.

Throughout the lengthy proceedings, Howard stood in the improvised dock, without a trace of emotion on his face. His uniform was crumpled from having been slept in for so many days. One epaulette had been torn off. His hair had not been combed and there was a stiff growth of beard on his face. The bright lights of the court-room made him blink until he got used to them. But his bearing was unchanged. He stood without flinching as the hours passed, and the appalling evidence built up. It was clear that he had no doubts about the outcome, that he regarded the trial as a quite unnecessary procedure; something merely to give his execution the veneer of justice. When Council for the Prosecution addressed him, he had three unchanging answers to the questions: 'I am a soldier', 'I was carrying out my orders' and 'I did my duty'. He gave the same answers to his own Council. Beyond this he would say nothing.

By midday, the courtyard outside the building was packed with people. They were in a ferment. They climbed on the roofs of parked cars to try to see through the windows. Speakers stood up from time to time on boxes, or were lifted above the surrounding heads by their supporters, and made violent and impassioned speeches. Banners made of sheets, fluttered in the slight breeze, carrying unequivocal messages: 'Hang Howard', 'Butcher of Nottingham', 'Remember the Dead' and the like. From time to time, a rumble of raised voices seemed to generate spontaneously at one point of the crowd and built into a shattering and prolonged roar. The sheer volume of noise seemed sufficient to bring the Debtors' Prison toppling down in dust. Stones were slung at the windows and glass shattered into the corridors above. Students who had brought up a length of heavy wood, began using it as a battering ram against the solid door and had to be driven back by the guards at bayonet point. Tear gas broke up the crowd from time to time, but it dispersed too quickly to keep them at bay for long. They were too incensed to be held back. They reformed, and crushed back into the courtyard area, more determined to get at Howard than ever.

Inside, sandwiches were served in the court-room for lunch. The proceedings moved forward into the afternoon. Fitzwallace listened carefully to every piece of evidence, but only Blackett seemed able to preserve his concentration quite unbroken. As time went on, he seemed to be relishing, if not actually enjoying, the proceedings. It seemed that he had a permanent, secret smile constantly inside him, that showed only in his eyes. By half-past three, the atmosphere inside the room had become so oppressive that Wordsworth, buoyed up though he was, by the thought of Jackman's determination, still found himself slipping from time to time into a light doze, from which he kept waking with a mild start. The windows were closed to keep out the noise from the front of the building. He had been smoking a succession of small cigars, and the heavy blue smoke hung motionless above the table. Still the proceedings bore on. Then, like a sudden burst of air and reality, a guard rushed into the room and told Fitzwallace that the front door had been broken down and the crowd was being contained in the stone entrance corridor. Fitzwallace rapped his stick on the table, suspended the proceedings and strode out with Blackett just behind him. The rest of the court got up and moved about the room to ease the tension that had built up through the long period of sitting and listening. Howard continued to stand unflinching in the dock. Jackman was standing, his right hand deep in his pocket. He seemed to be wondering whether this was the moment. Wordsworth caught his eye and nodded gently. From somewhere below there was a brief clatter of automatic fire. The sound seemed to be a cue for Jackman. He walked determinedly across the room and out of the door. No one but Wordsworth seemed to notice him. Certainly no one tried to stop him. The corridor outside was empty. From below Fitzwallace was shouting: 'Get them out! Drive them out! Stay outside, you men, and keep them clear of the door. Shoot if you must. Now get that door closed. Close it!' There were two or three single shots and then the grinding of the door to. In a moment there were steps on the stairs and Fitzwallace appeared from below, with Blackett and a guard immediately behind him.

'I want to see you,' said Jackman, standing at the top of the stairs.

'Later,' said Fitzwallace, brushing him to one side.

'Now', said Jackman, catching his sleeve as he passed.

'I told you later,' said Fitzwallace, trying to snatch his arm free.

Jackman got the pistol clear of his pocket and pointed it at Fitzwallace. He held the pistol as if he had never had one in his hand before. It didn't look very menacing. But the look in his eyes was fanatical. Fitzwallace realized in a moment that he had been screwing himself up to this for some long time. He could see from Jackman's expression that there was nothing impulsive about the action. He remembered the confrontation he had had with Jackman after the St. Martin's Lane massacre, the look in his eyes then, the unmovable determination. He knew that unless he did something quickly, Jackman would pull the trigger. He struck at the pistol with his stick and as he did so, Jackman fired. The roar was deafening in the close confines of the corridor. It boomed away into the distance as the bullet struck Fitzwallace and spun him away to the left, so that he hit the wall with his shoulder, lost his balance and fell. Blackett had no weapon. As Jackman stepped forward towards Fitzwallace, he picked up Fitzwallace's stick withdrew the sword blade from within, and plunged it deep into Jackman's side. It seemed an age before Jackman reacted to the thrust. He took a step away from Blackett, looked down at the length of blade protruding from his side, and then fixed his eyes on Blackett. There was a look of total incomprehension on his face, as if he had expected Blackett to applaud his action. He looked as if he was about to speak, and then changed his mind. He tilted over until his right shoulder rested against the wall and then, without taking his eyes off Blackett, he slid slowly down to the floor.

The sound of the shot brought two guards clattering up the

stone stairs. 'Colonel Fitzwallace has been injured,' said Blackett. 'Take him to his room. Then get this carcase out of the way.'

'Fortunately,' said Blackett, back in the court-room, 'Colonel Fitzwallace had the sense to wear protective clothing. I warned him some imbecile might try to remove him. The injury's not serious. As Vice-President of this court I shall continue the proceedings.' Wordsworth, who had taken up a position immediately behind the Presidential chair when the shot was fired, with the intention of taking command when Fitzwallace's death was announced, was taken too completely by surprise to challenge Blackett's statement. Before he had recovered his senses, Blackett was in the chair and the court was again in session.

The proceedings did not last for long. Blackett saw no point in letting the course of justice run at its natural pace. He ruled out much evidence that both parties wished to offer. In half an hour he was asking the Committee of Justice to bring in a verdict. He left it in no doubt what he thought that verdict had to be. Howard stood and listened to the verdict, as he had listened to everything else. It seemed to make no impression on him whatever. It looked as if the proceedings would finish in a moment with the brief passing of the sentence by Blackett. Everyone was hot and tired. Most people felt sick at what had been revealed during the trial, of Howard's ruthlessness and savagery. Many felt that a formal execution would hardly make up for Nottingham. Cries from the crowd outside still reached the court-room from time to time. Certainly no one was prepared for Blackett's incredible sentence. As he stood up he leaned forward over the table, resting the knuckles of his hands on it. He seemed to speak from a deep well of personal bitterness. Yet there was a certain satisfaction in the way he spoke. 'General Sir Maxwell Howard,' he snarled, scarcely opening his mouth for the words to escape, 'for the crime you have committed against the people of Nottingham no diabolical torture could be too great. The deaths of twenty-thousand people are on your head. I feel ill at being on the same earth with you. If there is a final justice, then I've never seen a man more eternally damned than you. You stand there hated and despised by mankind. You will be taken from this court to your cell. In the morning we shall hang you publicly.' He brought down his gavel sharply on the table and said: 'The proceedings are closed.'

'Did he say *publicly*?' said someone, as if he doubted his ears.

'Does he mean actually *in public*?'

'There's been no public hanging here for a hundred years! It's a monstrous idea!'

As Blackett made for one of the doors into the ante-room, he was caught by Fisher of the Committee of Justice. 'What kind of savages are we Blackett?' cried Fisher. 'What's the point of a spectacle like this?'

'We're all kinds of savages,' growled Blackett, thrusting his arm away. 'Can't you hear them? Can't you hear the savages growling outside?' Through the open door of the ante-room, the deep rumble of the crowd outside, like distant guns, was clearly audible. 'Do you think they'd let us hang him in private? They want blood. They'd tear the place down and all of us with it. Like wolfhounds, they need feeding. Well we'll feed them.' He pushed past Fisher and into the room beyond. A guard closed the door behind him. Another came up to him, saluted, and put the execution order in front of him to sign. It had been typed out before the trial began. He inserted the word 'publicly' and then signed the document. 'Get a loud-hailer,' he said. 'Read it to them from the window. Make sure they understand. And get hold of Patterson. He knows the building. We've got to keep Howard away from the crowd. They'll tear him to pieces. Everything's to be ready for inspection by 7 in the morning.'

Fitzwallace had been struck full in the left side of the chest. His armoured waistcoat had prevented penetration of the bullet, but the steel scales had been severely buckled, bruising his ribs. It was a little painful for him to breathe. Blackett found him in his drawing room, two of his guards sitting near him. What was upsetting him more than the pain, was the ingratitude he saw in Jackman's act. 'I've worked for them night and day,' he was saying. 'I've never spared myself. No one's seen me let up for one single moment since this thing began. And then this . . .'

'The trial's over,' said Blackett. 'Howard's been sentenced.'

'Where's Jackman? Where's that damned traitor?'

'Dead,' said Blackett.

'What!' cried Fitzwallace, getting to his feet. 'Before he could give any explanation?'

'I killed him. The gun was still loaded. He was going to make sure of you a second time.'

'Then I shall never know,' said Fitzwallace bitterly. He went to the window and looked out. He seemed to see nothing. He was totally preoccupied inside himself. At last he seemed to pull himself together again. He shrugged and turned from the window. He picked up the monocle from where it dangled on the end of the black ribbon, and screwed it into his eye. 'Well. The execution order's signed?'

'Yes.'

'And the announcement made?'

'Yes.'

'It's important to keep the people away from him.'

'Listen to them. They'll tear the place down.'

'They'll tear him to pieces.'

'Better that than the other.'

'Perhaps,' said Fitzwallace, his hand pressed against his chest. 'If we gave him to them, do you think?'

'They'd love that, wouldn't they. Wouldn't they just love that! Can't you see them pulling him to pieces—limb from limb like a fly?'

'What do you suggest?' asked Blackett. 'If we announce his execution, do you think they'll be satisfied?'

'My God,' said Fitzwallace. 'Can't we get away from this noise?'

'Hang him publicly,' said Blackett, putting the suggestion as if it had just occurred to him.

'What kind of animal are you Blackett?'

'A Northerner,' said Blackett.

'Yes. A black and savage place this North of *yours*.'

'Of *ours*.'

'Look,' said Blackett, walking over to him and looking him straight in the eyes. He looked to Fitzwallace like some form of human bulldog, with his chin thrust forward and his shoulders hunched. 'It makes no difference to Howard how he dies. Personally I'd throw him out of the window now, down into the midst of them. What do I care for Howard and his kind? If they see him swinging on the end of a rope, it'll take the edge off their appetite. They want blood—his or ours.'

'Oh God,' said Fitzwallace sitting down in an armchair. 'See to it,' he said at last. 'I want no part of it.'

Olsen elbowed his way through the crowd that surged down into Tower Street, and ran all the way back to the flat. He had moved out of his rooms in the Debtors' Prison, two days after his talk with Fitzwallace, and taken a flat at the corner of Fishergate and Paragon Street with Mrs. Paine.

'Darling, look at yourself,' she said, as he burst into the lounge. She pushed the hair away from his forehead and straightened his tie.

'They're hanging Howard in public in the morning!' he cried.

'It can't be true,' she said. 'You've made a mistake.'

'Blackett signed the execution order. They read it out from the window.'

'Not Fitzwallace?'

'He must be at the back of it. Blackett couldn't do it without him. What's happened to him? This is senseless—savage. Sheer brutal revenge. Brutish—brutish. I never understood him—that man.'

'The crowd—is it still there?.

'The whole town, I think. Packed together into the courtyard. Screaming, shouting for blood, hammering on the door of the headquarters. I don't know how long the soldiers can hold them off. If they get in . . . poor Rubinstein, I'd forgotten he's still in there. And I let Fitzwallace put him there. What he stood for, I stand for you know. I thought he was weak with his liberal principles and talk of justice. An old man. He wasn't.

That screaming mass of people there—that's weakness. Weakness is the brute. Strong men—Rubinstein—have sensitivity of the soul.'

'Sit down. There's nothing you can do now.'

'There is. I must be there in the morning. I must shout out against it.'

'You can't darling. Stay here. Stay with me until it's over. In the present mood who'd listen to you?'

'It's not a question of making anyone listen. I don't expect them to listen. I don't really care whether they listen or not. But I care if this happens in the eyes of God and no one stands up naked and protests. I care if it's recorded in the history books that no one protested. It's a sin against the universe. There must be a man there to shout out against it. I can't change things, I know that. They'll hang Howard before the whole stinking town, whatever I say. But there must be a living voice there to cry out against it. If not, then what are we, we humans? Nothing! Dirt and bestiality—nothing.'

They lit fires during the night in the courtyard and up the slopes of Clifford's Tower. The night was balmy, starry. They had no need of the heat, but the flames and the activity of keeping the fires going, kept alight the tension. Through the night there were cries as a light appeared or was extinguished in one of the windows of the Prison itself. Groups gathered to watch the guard being changed every two hours. Someone let off a rocket that swooshed into the air, then burst into an umbrella of brilliant little lights high overhead. On the steps of the Castle Museum, a man sat with a little group round him, playing softly on a mouth-organ.

Before dawn, ripples of excitement ran through the crowd as the rumours spread that the scaffold was being erected on the site of the old eight-o'clock walk and gallows, overlooking St. George's Field at the back of the Prison. There was a general movement of people in that direction. When Olsen got there at 4 a.m., he could hear the penetrating clatter of hammers on wood before he rounded the corner, and the cry and babble of the crowd and the cheers as a new wooden member was nailed into position. Olsen tried to push into the swaying mass of people towards the structure, only to be thrust out each time. On the traffic island a vast bonfire burned, throwing up dense and acrid smoke from scorching car-tyres. The light from it projected vast, grotesque shadows of people on the blank prison wall. Shadows of the scaffold ran to the top of the wall. Parents were lifting children up on their shoulders to see it. There was no control of any kind. No troops, except for those guarding the prison itself. No police, except for a constable watching the fire to see that it didn't get out of control. A number of drunks rolled down Tower Street from the direction of the police station. When they found they couldn't get past the crowd, they stood and chanted: 'We want Howard! We want Howard!' One of them, bored at last with the chanting, turned and kicked in the window of a sweetshop.

By six o'clock, people were arriving from outside the town in cars. By seven, more than thirty coaches had arrived from the West Riding and were parked along the length of Bishop-thorpe Road. Nothing crossed Skeldergate Bridge because of the crowd. On the far side of the river, people had taken up positions on the old Norman mound of Baille Hill, with telescopes and binoculars. The scene had a festive atmosphere, an atmosphere of gaiety and lightheartedness. Olsen thought: This is my species. I belong to this form of life. People sat on the wall of the bridge, eating sandwiches and drinking hot tea and coffee out of flasks. A few had brought bottles of beer. It could scarcely have been a better day for an outing, with the sun already warm and the sky blue and cloudless and the air full of summer perfumes. Olsen heard a woman say to her two children: 'Behave yourselves till it's over, then I'll take you on the river.'

An ice-cream van took up a position on the far side of Skel-dergate Bridge, its chiming bell penetrating the morning, reverberating from the solid wall of warehouses that rose up out of the river. A hot-dog man set up his barrow by the corner of Peckitt Street. Papers smeared in mustard, drifted down the street towards the river. Then, like a burst of local thunder, came the throbbing of the band of the Railway Institute. All

163

heads turned towards Clifford Street. In the distance, people were moving on to the pavements to let it pass. And it came into sight at last with a gallant roar of trumpets and trombones, booms and clatters of drums and cymbals, and the deep oomp-oomp-oomp of tubas and Sousaphones. At the head, a man dressed in a leopard skin was tossing a mace into the air. It flew up, turned in the polished light of morning, hung for a moment and then dropped back into his hand. The man never looked at it. It seemed to be on a string, so certain was the man that it would fall squarely into his waiting hand. Windows opened down the length of Tower Street. People held children on the sills so they could see. A man in pyjamas pushed his grizzled head out and shouted: 'Do you have to make that bloody noise? I'm on nights!'

Valerie lay awake, waiting for Olsen to come back. She knew there was nothing she could do to prevent his going out, down there into that rabble. For a time she believed that he would come back. She said to herself: There's nothing he can do. When he sees that, he'll come back. But he didn't come back. The distant noise of the crowd, the penetrating chime of the ice-cream bell, the rumble of the band grew. She began to be frightened. The air seemed full of bats' wings, fluttering, swooping, weaving across the sun. She thought: This is the way the world will end, with the sun high, and the noise, and the air filled with little creatures. If ever I was in love it was with this man. She had a sudden terrifying premonition— a vision almost, it was so brilliant and clear—that she would not live beyond the day. Something in her was in terrible danger. She got up and put on a dressing gown and slippers and ran out into the street. No one noticed her, thrusting her way through the crowds moving down Fishergate to the place of execution. She fought, pushing and beating against the crammed bodies; then at last she could go no further. She was jammed in that swaying human sea, bruised where she had been caught by an elbow or a swinging hand, pressed on so closely that she couldn't raise her arms from her sides. She managed to raise herself on to her tiptoes, but there was no sign of Olsen, only the shifting heads and children on shoulders unable to get down again, and over to the right a furled umbrella stuck up in the air. And there in front was the scaffold draped in red cotton cloth and with the flag of the North hanging limply over it. Then she saw Olsen, his back to the Prison wall, trying to force himself forward to where a line of guards stood before the scaffold. She shouted and shouted. Every time she emptied her lungs she had to fight to fill them again, against the human pressure upon her. She freed an arm and waved, but no one took any notice. She felt the tears streaming down her face. She was held like a moth impaled on a setting-board, entirely impotent. She seemed to weep for all the occasions in the past when she had felt nothing.

It was a quarter to eight. The door from the old unshackling yard opened and six trumpeters in scarlet tabards appeared. They walked up the rising ground and on to the scaffold. There they stood in a line and blew a long sad fanfare. The sudden solemnity of the moment, quietened the crowd. There was a sense of being in church, a religious sense. The ice-cream chimes stopped. Some men removed their hats. A catholic woman crossed herself and gave the slightest of genuflections. The hot-dog man closed the flap on his barrow and folded his arms to watch. A few children, feeling the mass tension, began to cry. One little boy, sitting high on his father's shoulders, said loudly: 'When's the horses?' and people near him laughed gently. A woman with heavy jowls and her hair in plastic curlers turned to her husband and said: 'That kid—what's it say?' 'It says "When's the horses?" ' said her husband. 'Shh!' said someone.

Four guards with automatic weapons appeared and behind them Blackett with a black cowl over his shoulders. Behind him walked a giant of a man, his head and face hidden inside a black hood. At the sight of him there was a long intake of breath from the crowd, that sounded like the rustle of wind through ripening wheat. Blackett stepped to the front of the scaffold, brushing aside the dangling rope as he did so. A guard handed him a loud-hailer and he whistled into it to make sure that it was working. One or two people laughed at the odd sound it produced. Blackett had no sense of the dramatic, no sense of the occasion. He stood hunched before the crowd, the loud-hailer to his mouth like a vast extension of his chin, and made the baldest of statements.

'Fellow Northerners,' he boomed, turning from one side of the crowd to the other, 'we're here to hang a man. A loathsome man. The Nottingham Butcher!' There were angry cries and boos. 'I want you to witness this, because I don't want it to be said afterwards that this is a piece of personal vengeance. It's not. It's an expression of our revulsion as Northerners against this man, against those who sent him and against that smoky wen for which he stands. Show him just what we think of him and his kind.'

There were mixed boos and cheers as Blackett stepped back off the scaffold. A tuba player blew a long raspberry on his instrument. The sense of solemnity evaporated. Through the open door into the unshackling yard, a clergyman could be seen hovering before making his appearance, and behind him three or four darker figures. Then Howard, his hands roped together behind him, was pushed forward through the doorway. He stopped and looked round, blinking in the bright sunlight. The crowd roared and tried to move forward, filling every tiny space with humanity. The Railway Institute Band struck up with the Northern Anthem played in quick march time. People burst into the chorus. The volume of sound rising from the comparative silence, seemed as if it would shatter the stones that had stood for centuries. The noise was a palpable pressure more than sound. It seemed to rise like a bomb-blast from the earth and reverberate from the very dome of heaven. Valerie got her hands to her ears. She could hear herself screaming and screaming, but could do nothing to prevent herself. She dare not close her eyes. She had to look, to keep her eyes on the morning light, lest she sank into that perpetual darkness that lurked at the edge of her field of vision. She saw Olsen break through the cordon of guards and reach the scaffold. She heard him begin to shout, 'No! No! No! No! No!' then 'Stop!' He was waving his arms for silence, but the noise simply increased. No single word was discernible, simply the crash of voices growing louder and louder. Then someone reached up over the edge of the scaffold and seized him by the leg. Another hand came up, then another and another. They dragged him to the edge of the scaffold and he stood there for a moment, pleading, protesting, waving his arms. Then he overbalanced into the front ranks of the crowd and disappeared from Valerie's sight. There was a disturbance where he had fallen, and then no more.

It had been a matter of a moment. A diversion from the main purpose. A brief curtain-raiser. Most of the crowd had not heard a word he had said. Some had not even noticed the incident. The roars and the rousing music of the band were unchanged. The ice-cream bell joined in. Children began to wave little Northern flags, as Howard walked to the noose. He walked of his own free will. No one pushed him. No one forced him. There was a certain dignity—majesty almost—about his bearing. It seemed to infuriate the crowd. 'Hang the bastard!' someone shouted. 'String him up!' The mouth-organist tried to play the Chopin Funeral March, but someone knocked the instrument out of his mouth and it was crushed beneath the feet of the crowd. As the hangman tried to fit the noose over his head, people began pulling at the scaffold. They ripped away the red drapery. Half a dozen began to climb the wood-work on to the platform. Guards ran forward and knocked them back. But others were gaining a foothold and the guards were outnumbered. 'Let's get at him,' shouted a young man who had got his hands on the loud-hailer, and twenty more clawed their way up the wooden framework. The guards fired over the heads of them, but it was too late. The hangman was knocked over. The guards retreated towards the open door. The clergyman, trying to protect his glasses, had his surplice torn off. The crowd had its hands on Howard. He was being punched and kicked, his hands still fastened behind his back. There was nothing he could do to protect himself. And then he was thrown off the platform into the main mass of the crowd. As he fell on them, they tore at him with their hands, and as he fell below the level of their hands they kicked him with their feet. There were screams and shouts of jubilation, and then as the violent edge of passion wore off, they lifted up the battered bleeding body for everyone to see.

Valerie found herself lying on the pavement. The crowd had gone. Only its droppings remained; the drifting hot-dog papers, the empty cigarette packets, the crushed sandwiches and broken bottles. As she moved she ached. She sat on the edge of the pavement, her head buried in her knees. When she looked at herself she found that her dressing gown and night-dress were torn. She had lost her slippers, and her right foot had been crushed under someone's heel. When she got up, she found it difficult to stand on it. There was in the back of her mind a distracted thought that something urgent must be done. Across the road lay the shattered woodwork of the scaffold. The red drapery had gone. The flagpole had been smashed. Bodies lay among the debris. On the slope of Clifford's Tower, a man staggered as if he were drunk. His left arm hung shattered from his shoulder, the whole sleeve soaked in blood. And then she remembered. She remembered the dreadful feeling of choking under the weight of all those bodies pressing against her, and the trumpets and the band, the boom of Blackett's voice over the loud-hailer and the sight of Olsen being dragged off the platform and sucked down into the whirlpool of the crowd. And she limped across the road, forgetting the pain in her foot, not noticing the showers of broken glass that lay everywhere. But there was no sign of him near the scaffold. She ran up the hill to the Prison entrance and battered with her fists on the door. A grille opened and a puffed, unshaven face looked through at her. 'Olsen,' she said. 'Where is he?' 'Go away,' growled the face. She battered on the heavy woodwork again and cried: 'Where is he?' 'Don't know him,' said the face. 'Clear off.' 'Let me in. Let me see Colonel Fitzwallace.' 'Stop chipping that paintwork,' he said, 'and put some clothes on—you look like a whore from Twickenham.'

The grille slammed to. No amount of hammering brought it open again. She looked up at the windows above, but there was no movement there. The mess over the courtyard was unbelievable. Newspapers lay trampled into the grass of the central island, together with half-eaten sausages and sandwiches and bottles. Someone had left a child's blue carry-cot on the steps of the Assize Courts with a blue shawl and pillow inside it and a big multicoloured rattle tied to one of the handles. She ran distracted to the steps of the Castle Museum, but there was no sign of Olsen. She ran through the carpark, looking in the few parked vehicles as she went. Every living thing seemed to have disappeared. On the far side of Clifford's Tower she came across the hot-dog barrow lying on its side, the contents spilled over the road. The hot-dog man sat propped against the wall of the fire-station. When she shook him he groaned, but he was too injured to speak.

Back at the scaffold she began frantically pulling away the woodwork. Her hands were covered with blood from pulling clear the dead bodies. As she pulled away a cracked prop, the platform tilted down towards her. It looked as if it might collapse at any moment. The body of a man that had been lying on the platform, slithered off and fell at her side, totally relaxed in death. She was on her hands and knees under the creaking platform. It was dark. The air seemed damp and stagnant. It was a place without sun. She found the red cotton drapery where it had been pushed under the platform and behind it the body of Olsen.

It took her some time to ease it out into the sun from under the platform. She tried to lift it, but it was too heavy for her. She was crying, not with sorrow, but with chagrin at her inability to cope with the weight. At last she managed to drag it clear of the other carnage and lay it half way up the grass slope that ran to the wall of the Prison. There she bent to look at what was left to her of Olsen. His chest was crushed where he had been trampled on. On one side of his head was a deep indentation where he had been kicked. His hair was matted with drying blood. She lifted his head in her arms. Her tears fell on his face. 'Dear dead face,' she said, brushing the matted hair off his forehead and kissing him on the bruised lips. There was no small spark of life left in them. Not the smallest answering pressure, not the least unconscious tremor that she could have succoured against her breast and warmed and nurtured back into life. He was gone from her irretrievably. She felt a supreme, superhuman sense of anger against God and all his works. The inhumanity of God! she thought. And then the sense of utter impotence, the knowledge that she could do nothing whatever about it. She beat the earth with her fists in impotent fury, but it merely bruised her. She thought: 'If I wait a moment I'll hear a voice from heaven call out: "This is one of my sons, Sidney Olsen, in whom I am well-pleased." ' But there was no voice, except her own mutterings in her ears. The sky above was clear. No gathering of thunder clouds and rending of the fabric of heaven for this man's death. No symbolic dove. No hopeful rainbow. 'All the theatrical panoply of heaven for *your* son,' she thought. 'For mine—for my lover—just another sunny day.' She shouted at the sky: 'Selfish, wicked bastard!'

She laid his head gently back on the grass and stood up. She looked at the blood on her hands and dressing gown. She remembered the premonition of the early morning. Indeed, something of the very essence of her had withered and died.

A police car drew up on the road and a constable called: 'You all right, Miss?'

'I'm all right,' she said.

'They'll be collecting the bodies in a minute. This one yours?'

'No,' she said, 'it's not mine. Bury it with the rest of them.'

Paine had heard nothing from his wife since that night in June when she had left for the North. For some days he had thought nothing of it. He was used to her disappearances. Besides, the vast quantities of work he was now expected to get through, left him almost no time for reflection. Most of the time, he slept in his office on a metal-framed campbed. On the few occasions when he went to the flat, it seemed no more empty than usual.

And yet, despite what their relationship might appear on the surface, it was nonetheless a relationship. There was something between them. A tie, a link. They were not simply two people living together for the sake of material convenience. It was not, of course, 'love'. Not the desire of the moth for the star. Not a ubiquitous, burning passion. But it was a bond and he felt incomplete without it. She was unreliable in the conventional sense, and yet there was a predictability about her to Paine. After three weeks, he knew that she was either being prevented from getting a message through; alternatively she was dead. Perhaps she had never got through at all. Perhaps she had been dead for weeks already. Perhaps he had been waiting for a communication that could not possibly come. Certainly, by mid-July he was trying hard to reconcile himself to never hearing from her or seeing her again. At times in the past, he had seriously considered getting rid of her. When he had had a brief affair with that secretary from the American Embassy, with the seedy little flat in Notting Hill, it had been a rather elaborate attempt to show his wife that they could not possibly continue living together. He had it all worked out. Divorce wasn't necessary. He had no intention of marrying again. He was quite prepared to make a financial settlement on her, though certainly she had no need of money. But when he put it to her she simply laughed. 'Not a bit of it,' she said. 'Life with you suits me. In any case I couldn't give up a *pied à terre* in London.' Such memories made it all the more difficult for him to account for his present deep sense of loss.

'I know how you feel, Robert,' the PM told him. 'I've relations of my own in the North. But there's nothing you can do about it. Mustn't let it interfere with your work, not at a time like this. Couldn't do without you, you know.'

But of course he didn't know how Paine felt, and Paine knew it. He didn't believe he was indispensable either. He wondered more why he kept going than how. At the end of it a present from the Department and a knighthood if he behaved himself. And then retirement alone to Bosham or Broadstairs. And somebody down there would make quite a thing about having a knight living next door—Sir Robert Paine.

But things were deteriorating. Work piled up for Paine and everyone else. There was feverish diplomatic activity to keep a check on. The PM had still not succeeded in persuading the Norwegians and Danes to cut off food supplies to Newcastle and Hull. Indeed, relations with the Scandinavian countries had deteriorated. They felt a bond with the North through a certain common ancestry. They too felt a little left out in the cold.

Then, as the full blousiness of summer fell on the South, the PM made the cryptic remark to Paine: 'It's no use Robert, we can't hold them ourselves. I'm calling on our principal allies for help.'

And indeed they couldn't be held. With a burst of unbelievable vigour and violence, the Northern armies had penetrated the

Home Counties. No one who saw them coming could ever forget the sight. They came on foot and in lorries, they came in tanks and by air, the medium and fighter-bombers softening the path in front of them, over the undulating country of Buckinghamshire and Hertfordshire. Resistance, incredibly brave in places, eventually crumbled before them. One spearhead in fast armoured cars, penetrated as far as the main street of Cricklewood causing devastation with flame-throwers and firebombs. In the west, the Welsh had overrun Rickmansworth and Uxbridge, and were picking at the outskirts of Ruislip. People fled before them, as people had fled in the past before Genghis Khan. And then suddenly they were held. Partly it was their exuberant lack of discipline, that made them an increasingly easy target for the organized Southern forces. But there was another, much more important factor, a factor that played a decisive role in the final outcome of the war.

General Quigley was standing outside his temporary headquarters in a field near Potters Bar, watching the bombardment of defended positions in Barnet, when a runner brought him a signal. It read: 'Northern cities heavily bombed this morning by B.254 aircraft of American 12th Airforce. Heavy armour reported landed Dover, Folkestone, Deal. Expect to encounter substantial American reinforcements within next twenty-four hours.'

10

THE first American advance, with heavy armour and massive air support, broke the Welsh line between Farnham and Guildford and rolled the eastern edge of the breech northwards towards Windsor. After two days of bitter fighting, the Welsh were in disorganized retreat. In three days they had been broken completely. Cardiff and Swansea had been heavily bombed. Most of the small industrial towns in the south of Wales had been hit. News of the bombing shattered the morale of the soldiers in the field. Harrassed by low-flying fighter aircraft, they moved back through the west country. American units pursued them over the border and up into the hills. Those who had been caught east and north of Guildford, were put in large barbed-wire compounds. Londoners travelled to compounds in Denham and Staines to throw stones at the prisoners through the wire.

Quigley lost 47 aircraft in his first encounter with American airpower. Raids on his headquarters and artillery positions forced him to abandon the bombardment of Barnet and consolidate to the north. The Battle of Ware raged for three days with appalling Northern losses of men and equipment. The Americans were fresh, magnificently equipped, and convinced that they were doing no more than suppress a local revolt over a legitimate government. They put tremendous heart into the flagging Southern troops. Success followed success. In London, parades in support of American intervention took place in Trafalgar Square and Hyde Park. In New York the papers were calling it 'The Holy War'.

More than anything, the bombing of Northern towns had a disastrous effect on morale. It seemed that the desert out of which the North had just been climbing, had returned overnight. Manchester was a smoking mess after two days of continuous bombing. Piccadilly was a vast waste of rubble. A good deal of the new university building had been destroyed. Acres of new flats had disappeared in Leeds and Bradford. The Queen's Hotel and the new City Station were no more than shells. All the new development in Forster Square was devastated in a single raid. The grimmest realization was that Southern capital would again be needed to repair the damage. 'They'll come up here,' said a taxi-driver, looking down on Bradford from the ring-road, 'with their bloody Christian charity and Southern construction firms and build it up again. Then they'll expect us to love them for another thousand years.'

Nothing escaped. To the tacticians in London everything Northern was a legitimate target. Nothing was worth preserving. That savagery and bitterness that has always characterized civil war, directed military thinking. By comparison with the raids on Hull, Newcastle and Manchester, the raids on York were not heavy. But their effect was devastating. The whole medieval city was gutted between 10 and 10.12 in the morning. One side of Coney Street, with the Herald Offices, bookshops and stores, was pushed clean into the river. The Guildhall, rebuilt after the bombing of 1942, was destroyed. The Mansion House and the Assembly Rooms ceased to exist, and almost the only thing recognizable in Stonegate was the signboard of *Ye Olde Starre Inne,* that still swung crazily over the street. Two bombs plunged through the roof of the Minster and shattered the interior of the nave and choir. Priceless stained glass lay scattered over the lawns and the road. The head verger sat in tears in the crypt as the entire west wall of the cathedral collapsed, crushing the first houses in Precentor's Court.

In a sense, Jackman's bullet had done its work. Fitzwallace had lost his grip on the situation long enough for Blackett to push him from power. He was confined to his room under guard at the time of the bombing. The first bombs to fall in the area of the Debtors' Prison demolished the unshackling yard and tore a hole in the stonework of Fitzwallace's room. Through this he dropped down on to the mound of rubble and hid until the bombardment was over. From there, during the chaos of fires and toppling buildings, he reached the river. Some of the rowing boats tied up for the tourist traffic, were still afloat. He climbed into one, undid the painter and pulled away downstream.

Blackett seemed to have lost all sense of the position. He was convinced that the bombing was an isolated sting in the dying tail of the South. He issued impossible orders to his closest commanders. One man was shot on the spot for questioning the thinking behind them. He could be seen, in the days before the bombardment, striding about the building, wearing the armoured waistcoat he had taken from Fitzwallace, brandishing a 9 m.m. Browning automatic in the face of anyone he met. Water, gas and electricity supplies to the City were cut off. All bridges over the river had gone, so that one side of the City was completely separated from the other. The crowds that had so recently howled with Blackett at the execution of Howard, now howled against him. Looting was an occurrence of almost every minute, now that a man need do no more than pick his way through a pile of rubble to find what he wanted. The total social disintegration that followed the air-raids, brought with it an almost total moral disintegration too. No one was safe alone in the streets. Armed gangs walked the town robbing and killing their neighbours, smashing whatever stood in their way, adding destruction to devastation as if in revolt against everything the hand of man had ever made. The church of St. Mary in Castlegate, which had miraculously escaped the bombing, was burnt to the ground during the early days of August. Its vast immaculate spire collapsed into dusty rubble, for no better reason than that it had continued to stand, a significant creative shape above the ruins, in defiance of bedlam.

Fitzwallace put ten miles of river between himself and the City of York, before he pulled to the bank. It was hot. He sat on the bank for some time, looking over the water and over the flat countryside. The best of the year has passed, he thought. Spring was the time. Spring, yellow with new growth, and life surging up again from the earth. Spring, before all this terrible business began. Spring, when the idea had still been lit with enthusiasm and idealism—a march for a new world, a march into the sunlight of summer. But it had turned bitter. They could say that it was the dissension at the top, at the seat of power. No doubt they would say it. But it wasn't that at all. It was something in the Northern spirit that wasn't in essence independent. It could rise in a bloody bubble of fury, but it couldn't take charge. It couldn't see itself in command. Generations of subservience had built servility into its very nature. Its soul was a peasant. And that old myth, thought Fitzwallace, about Northern bluntness and independence; how long would that be perpetuated? And what am I? An adventurer, too irresponsible to govern.

Now summer was passing. Blousy, dusty. The corn was ripening around him. The grass on the river bank had grown tall and rank. From the south came the rumble of guns. He walked through the hot afternoon, past Stillingfleet and Escrick. In Wheldrake he stole a bicycle that had been propped against the wall of the shop. Keeping to the unfrequented lanes, missing Elvington and Stamford Bridge, he reached Wordsworth's massive house by 6 o'clock.

He was shown into the library that contained not only books, but trophies of all kinds. There were the masks and brushes of innumerable foxes, together with twenty or more guns and pistols. Photographs of Wordsworth in various outdoor guises, hung about the room. He sat down in the enormous bay window and picked up a copy of *The Field*. But Wordsworth came before he had a chance to open it.

'So it's true,' shouted Wordsworth. 'I thought my man must be mistaken. I didn't think you'd have the damned gall to come here!'

'Well you were wrong. I had,' said Fitzwallace, turning in his chair to see him, but not getting up.

'So I see. By God you'll regret it.'

'Possibly. I'm beginning to regret it already. You were never the most congenial of company. But I've not come socially. I've come because it's over—we're finished. We've got to stop it now, before the whole land's decimated.'

'What! You've come to me for support! My God, after all the times you've refused to listen to my advice before. And now, when you can't control things any more you come crawling here expecting me to pull you out of the mire!'

'Not crawling, Wordsworth, I assure.'

He sat dangling one leg over the other, sunk deep into the chair. His apparent casualness infuriated Wordsworth.

'If not crawling, what then?' shouted Wordsworth.

'If you would stop shouting for a moment, perhaps I could tell you.'

'And take that damned affected monocle out of your eye before I smash it.'

'You're right, you know. It is affected. There's nothing at all the matter with my sight. In the early days I could never remember which eye to put it to. It's a habit, that's all. Do overlook it. But you know how habits grow. I can't break it now. I've had it too long.' He screwed the monocle very deliberately back into his eye. 'You smoke, I see.'

'Well?'

'Well there you are. You overlook my bad habit, and I'll overlook yours. The position is this: Blackett is a madman and will go on to the bitter end. In that case the North is finished. They won't leave one brick standing on another. Not even your place here. I thought that between us we might sue for peace. Between us we could raise enough support. If we could get that poor devil Rubinstein out of prison—if he's still alive —he'd support us too. We might just save something out of the ruins.'

'Sue for peace,' sneered Wordsworth. 'And what do you think they'll do with you in the South—throw their arms around you?'

'Oh no,' said Fitzwallace. 'They'll hang me. I expect that. But then, whatever the outcome, they'll hang me. I'm finished and I accept it. But we might save a lot more hanging if we approach them now.'

'You're finished all right,' said Wordsworth. He walked over to a little bureau and took a heavy revolver from the top drawer. He turned to Fitzwallace again and said: 'You're finished all right.'

'Your father's I imagine,' said Fitzwallace waving a finger towards the gun. 'From the Somme was it, or Passchendaele?' He got up as if extremely weary. 'Well,' he said, 'where would you like me to stand. Over by the door perhaps, where it'll be more convenient for your man to drag me out? Or by the window, where you can get a clearer view of me, silhouetted against the evening sky?' When Wordsworth said nothing Fitzwallace snapped irritably: 'Well for God's sake shoot man!'

'I should have done it myself weeks ago instead of letting that damn' fool Jackman make a mess of the job.'

'Ah, you put him up to that, did you?'

'Do you think he'd have the wit to think of it himself?'

'Yes, I believe he would, if you'd given him time. Do you know where we all went wrong, Wordsworth? We went wrong in having self-centred, self-opinionated, witless boors like you supporting us. We're not ready for manhood and maturity yet, because too many of us have your unimaginative zeal for self-advancement. Where do you differ from the scum of London? You have the same standards, the same values. You're a traitor in the Northern camp. You don't want freedom and liberation for the North, you want to bring London up here. You want the degradation of Soho and Paddington across your lawns. You want Regent Street to run through Gateshead to Tyne Bridge. Yes, I made a mistake, but it wasn't in refusing your advice. I knew well enough where that would lead. No, the mistake was in getting rid of Rubinstein and letting you go free. For Rubinstein is a Northerner with a passion for the liberation of people. But you—look at you—you are a fat, blighted maggot, not a whit better than the pigs you breed, and a damn' sight more ignoble than the foxes you've got hanging on your walls.'

Wordsworth was glistening with hatred, but still he didn't pull the trigger. It seemed as if he wanted to injure Fitzwallace with words before putting him permanently beyond injury. But no words came.

'Very well,' said Fitzwallace, 'if you can't, you can't.' He walked towards the door. As he turned the knob Wordsworth fired. The heavy bullet went straight through his chest and into the door. The force of the impact threw him face first against the woodwork. He seemed to cling to it for a moment, and then began to slither down it towards the floor. As he did so the monocle fell out of his dying eye and he breathed: 'In the—back. Well . . .'

Wordsworth decided to sue for peace himself, in his capacity as Chairman of the Council of the North. His chairmanship had been purely nominal for many weeks, but he gambled on the fact that the Southern authorities would not know this. His real motivation was the thought that something might still be saved for himself from the wreckage. If he were the principal means of restoring peace, then he might well be allowed to keep what he had. He might even add to it. As a Northerner, as a substantial landowner and industrialist, as a man who had been at the centre of power, there was every chance that he might be given control of the North under the central government. He had, he felt, a strong case. He had had no share in the decisions that Fitzwallace had taken, and Blackett had not even acknowledged his existence. He had got rid of Fitzwallace himself. Blackett alone was responsible for the continued resistance.

But the problem was to make contact with the Southern command. He had no radio transmitter. He had no one he could trust to bear his message to the South and not direct to Blackett. The roads would be impassable. He ordered a hunter to be saddled, and on the morning after the death of Fitzwallace, he set off across country to establish contact with the Southern forces.

From the top of Garrowby Hill, there was no difficulty in defining the forward positions. The rumble of distant guns filled the air. A pall of smoke hung over the countryside north of Selby and Howden. There was no doubt but that the Southern armies had crossed the Humber, the last obstacle to their invasion of East Yorkshire. To the south, Market Weighton was hidden behind the smoke. To the west, it appeared that they were already over the Ouse at Cawood. He rode along the western ridge of the Wold escarpment, and then dropped down into Pocklington. The roads north and east were choked with vehicles, trying to get away from the advancing armies. People on foot made better progress through the fields. Some carried children on their shoulders. Others had overloaded themselves with the most precious of their household belongings and now were having to jettison some of them. Wordsworth was surprised to see how many people were trying to carry mattresses away with them. Most of those on foot were making for the high ground of the Wolds. He drew up his horse by the side of a middle-aged man, struggling up the slope with an enormous roll of blankets on his back. 'Hey. You there,' he called. 'Are they in the town yet?'

'Didn't wait to see', said the man, continuing to climb the hill.

'Damn' well stand still when I talk to you,' shouted Wordsworth.

'All right,' said the man, 'let me put this lot on your horse and I'll stand still.'

'You damned impudent . . . !' cried Wordsworth, taking a cut at him with his crop.

Then, not a mile south of Pocklington, he saw the remnants of Quigley's 3rd Army pulling back. They looked like mechanical men in their tattered uniforms, moving stiffly towards the west and north. He rode into a group of them. Some were without helmets. Many had lost their arms. Their eyes stared ahead. They took no notice of him, walking past his horse as if they had not seen it. 'How far away are they?' he called from the saddle. One of them pointed to the south, but kept on walking.

Further south were the shell and bomb craters, where some brief stand had been made. The bombardment now was falling to the west, over towards Escrick on the Selby-York road. Along the road to York from Market Weighton, strings of burnt-out lorries sagged on their wheel-rims. The acrid smell of smoke hung over everything. Fields of ripening corn and late bales of hay had been set on fire by the bombardment. The ground was still hot and smouldering in places, and he had difficulty in forcing the horse to cross over it. A tiny wood still glowed with flame on his left. An isolated farmhouse and outbuildings lay shattered on his right. The carcasses of a dozen Friesian cows lay in the corner of a field under a smashed tree. Passing the ruined farm buildings he saw the bodies of the farmer and his family lying about the fold-yard amongst the remains of pigs and poultry. A hen ran clattering out and between the legs of his horse, flapping and screeching so that the horse rose in terror on its hind legs. An old sow, its back legs cut off by shrapnel, lay grunting painfully on top of the midden.

Then, past the increasing desolation and ruins of war, he got his first glimpse of a Southern patrol. There were twenty or thirty of them, moving crouched along the back of a hedge. He turned and pushed his horse towards them across the scorched stubble. They stopped and watched him. A young officer had binoculars to his eyes. Wordsworth lifted his crop and waved to them. When he was less than a hundred yards from them, one of them fired at him with a light machinegun. He felt the horse shudder beneath him as the bullets struck it, and then it dropped to its knees, its head slipping over to one side, and in a moment he found himself pitched over its neck and on to the hot earth. He lay there watching them. Two of them climbed through the hedge and came towards him, sub-machineguns covering him. They stood in front of him at last, trying to decide who he was.

'What the devil did you do that for? Didn't you see me wave?'

'Get up,' said one of them.

'Take me to your commanding officer,' he snapped, getting to his feet and brushing the earth and charred stubble off his jacket.

'Shut up,' said the soldier, putting the muzzle of his gun in his back and pushing him towards the rest of the patrol.

'So you're one of the bastards, are you?' said the young lieutenant.

'I'm Sir Brian Wordsworth,' said Wordsworth, standing up to his full height, 'Chairman of the Council of the North.'

'Are you, by God! Then I don't give a tuppenny toss for your chances.'

At Southern forward headquarters, Wordsworth was interviewed by a Brigadier, who strutted and puffed from one side of the tent to the other as he talked. 'I'd think you a brave man,' he said, hands clasped behind his back, eyes staring at the ground ahead of him, 'riding straight through the line like that. As it is, I know you're a bastard. If I'd any sense I'd have you butchered now, and your guts strung out from here to Liverpool. But that'll have to wait. They'll want a look at you in London. As for this peace offer, I take it it's some personal joke of yours. Frankly I fail to find it amusing. Let me tell you —Wordsworth—no one sues for peace in this war. You're all damned rebels—traitors. We'll treat you as such. We'll make an example of you. Before there's any talk of peace, we'll have every stick and stone in the North knocked down. I'll see to it there's not a woman that my men don't rape. There won't be a man that we don't shoot. There won't be a Northern child three weeks from now, who isn't glad to lick a Southern arse for a crust of bread. We'll sack your cities and burn your fields. We'll smash your factories and pull down your cathedrals. We'll carry your stones to Southend and build them into pleasure palaces for Londoners. And you and your stinking kind, we'll sell you in Hyde Park, and every Londoner will have two of you to wait on him, to clean his shoes and make his meals and trot behind his car. And nobody will remember the North. We'll erase it from human memory. We'll turn it into a dead wilderness that Christ himself would have boggled at. Peace, you damned Northerner! We'll show you what we mean by peace.'

Wordsworth was shackled hand and foot and thrown into the back of a Landrover. From there he was driven eventually to the Tower.

All humanity seemed to have evaporated. The normal rules of war had been suspended. There seemed no central policy of control or mercy. Perhaps it was that no such control was possible over victorious troops who felt that they were personally avenging the affront that the barbarians had inflicted on the South. Whatever town or village the Southern armies overran, they sacked and burnt. The bombing continued on every centre of population in the North. The Americans, increasingly under pressure from their own people to confine the bombing to obvious military targets, stepped up their efforts to bring the insurrection to a speedy conclusion. American bombing smashed the Northern cities. American ground forces destroyed the Northern armies, so that the armies of the South marched gloriously northwards, virtually unopposed. Wordsworth was hanged quietly in the Tower, the morning after his arrival, and before his peace petition could reach the authorities.

Valerie Paine forced her way down Fulford, against the crowds of refugees pushing blindly to the north. She was a ludicrous figure, if anyone had paused to notice her, dressed in the navy linen suit in which she had first travelled north, the ruby and diamond clasp still in position in the lapel of the jacket. She wore no make-up and carried no baggage. On her feet she wore broad-fitting flat-heeled shoes she had borrowed from a cleaner, since her own shoes would no longer fit her bruised and swollen feet. The shoes seemed to take all elegance out of her movement. She moved now, as she had never done in her life before, for no other purpose than to leave the place she was in and arrive at some other place. The town had become unendurable for her. The heat, the smell, the noise, the dust, the rumble of collapsing buildings under the bombardment. Disease was spreading rapidly through the remaining inhabitants. She clawed her way out in the only direction she knew— southwards. Tractors drawing trailers piled with household goods, filled the road. Dumb families, their arms hanging limp at their sides, pushed into town, staring straight ahead, knowing no better direction than forward. Occasional shells screamed overhead and crumped into the debris of York. From time to time one fell short. Ears had become attuned to the sound, and people dropped into the gutters or crouched like whipped curs in the doorways, until it had crashed into the roadway lifting tractors and lorries through house-fronts and splattering humanity over the walls. Then, without pausing, the uninjured got to their feet again and walked mechanically on. Northern troops were mixed with civilians, doctors from the Fulford Hospital moved shoulder to shoulder with cleaners from the sewage plant at Naburn. Everything had broken. Everything was disorder. All structure had gone.

She got into the fields outside the town, and the going was faster. The bombardment was still directed at the City, so that although shells passed high over her head, none fell near her. And at Crockey Hill, when she was beginning to think she could go no further, she ran into a soldier, little more than a boy she thought, who had lost contact with his patrol.

'Get back,' he said. 'You'll get yourself shot.'

'I'm a Southerner,' she said. 'I'm trying to get back to London.'

'How the hell you get up here?' he said.

'How can I get back?'

'Here, give me your hand. If they see you with me you might be all right. Trouble is, where the hell've they got to?'

She had a hard time at local headquarters, confronted by an aging Major who constantly ran his hands over her. 'Keep your filthy hands to yourself,' she said, the tears beginning to well up in her eyes. But she cried more with tiredness than injury. 'I'm pregnant.'

'I'll bet you are, darling. Full up with some little Northern bastard.'

'I'm the wife of Robert Paine, a secretary to the Prime Minister,' she said. 'I'll see that your conduct comes to the notice of the Army Council.'

Her words, and the authority that lay behind them, made him pause. A company sergeant-major took him aside and said in a whisper: 'Beg pardon, sir, but there was a signal a day or two back about some woman. This might be her. Wife of somebody or other in Whitehall.'

'Very well,' said the Major, clearly shaken but determined to make an effort at bluffing his way through. 'We've got to check everybody you understand. At a time like this, no knowing what rats and fifth-columnists might try to get through. Wouldn't do at all, would it? It'll take us a while to check your story. Meantime, sergeant-major, see about rustling up some tea.'

York was finally occupied on August 11th, the day the

Queen flew to Scotland for the grouse shooting. They found Blackett's body, still clutching a pistol in his hand, crushed beneath the masonry of the Debtors' Prison. Beside him were the bodies of three of his commanders, two of whom had been shot at close range.

In the ruins of the dungeons they found the bodies of prisoners. One or two had been shot. Most had died in the bombardment. Rubinstein had been crushed to death when part of the ceiling of the old condemned cell had collapsed. When they dragged his body out, they found a letter beneath it, that he had been writing to his wife with the thick stub of a pencil. It read:

My dearest Laura,

I think this may be a farewell letter to you, my dearest wife. We have been under continuous attack now for two days, and I do not think the building can last much longer. I have not spoken to anyone for some time, so I cannot tell the exact position. I am afraid things must be going badly for us.

I am tormented at times by the thought that I might have been wrong not to give them my full support when they asked for it. I really do not know whether it was cowardice or wisdom that made me hold back. But it seemed to me that to follow Fitzwallace blindly, would have been to lose sight of the ideals for which we were fighting. I did not think we could fight slavishly for freedom, and intolerantly for tolerance. But the outcome will make that clear to those who are left. And yet Fitzwallace is at heart a fine man, with so many of the finest attributes of the North in his spirit. I admire his courage and dash. I admire his colour in a countryside that is not notable for colour. I admire his spirit of adventure. Above all, I admire his ability to evoke love in those who serve him. And yet there is a final lack in him somewhere. A deficiency of some sort. I cannot exactly put my finger on it. It has to do with the nature of greatness. He lacks, perhaps, that wide, universal sweep of the imagination that sees each individual action against the vast backcloth of human history. An imagination that can see both the immediate implications of action, and at the same time the implications for generations unborn. There is a philosophical lack too, a lack of a permanent universal moral structure. It may seem unfair to make these judgements of a man at the very moment when he is embroiled in action. These are rare qualities, but there have been leaders in the world with them. Knowing your sense of fairness and justice, my dear Laura, let me hasten to say I do not blame him for any deficiency. It is not a man's own fault that he is born without one of the rarer qualities. Though I am here in prison at his command, I bear him no ill-will. What else could he have done? I left him no choice. Perhaps after all it is this that I am trying to say: there is in him a lack of a sense of history, a sense of destiny.

And you, my own dear wife, if we do not meet again, remember me with love. For I have loved you, and your love and kindness have given me strength and comfort every day of my life. I remember with deep pleasure how we first met at the Cohen's when poor Elizabeth was twenty-one, and how very beautiful you looked in your long pink dress under the chandeliers. I knew then that I was going to marry you, and if you wouldn't have me then I would marry no one. I remember how you have supported me through all the difficult times, and how we have shared together the pleasant ones. Life has been very good to me. I love you. The present will pass.

To the children all my love and affection. If Jessica's child is a boy, tell them for heaven's sake not to call him after me. Albert is not a name to be saddled with, though it has done me well enough.

If the worst comes to the worst, which I now fear, then I pray that this letter will be taken and delivered to you. And if, my dearest wife . . .

'Better give this to Lieutenant Black, don't you think?' said the soldier who had found the letter.

'For God's sake,' said his companion, 'at a time like this? Sling the bloody thing down and let's get out of here. You want the roof on your head?'

It seemed to her now like some horrific dream. She was standing at the window of the flat, looking down into the square. Nothing had changed, and yet she saw it through different eyes. A late thrush sang, hidden in the heavy foliage of a lime tree. The white flowers of the philadelphus bushes filled the air with perfume. There was an unreality about it; she felt like someone reliving part of childhood, but reliving it as an observer. Looking in upon it from outside, unable any longer to become involved in it, to become a part of it. An awful sense of nostalgia rose in her. Something had made it impossible for her ever to live this kind of sheltered life again. Superimposed upon the quiet, peaceful scene, like the superimposition of one picture on another in the cinema, was the memory of that dead and bleeding face she had uncovered from the debris of the scaffold. It was a memory that touched her to the very centre, and unfolded feelings that had been wrapped tight in her until that moment. She felt that somehow, in that particular death, the very quick of life had touched her. She would never be the same again.

Paine was saying from the room behind her: 'I think the end's in sight. Thank God it'll soon be over. The Americans are in Newcastle and our people are mopping up the coast.'

It was a week since her return, but she knew that whatever he said and whoever occupied what, it would never be over. Not in this way. In the midst of it all there were people, with individual aspirations and needs that could never be finally held by force, by the physical imposition of someone else's views upon them.

'I can't stay,' she said at last.

'Mm?' said Paine, still sitting in the chair behind her, papers on his knees and on the carpet in front of him.

'I must get away.'

'Of course,' he said, picking up his stick and pulling himself to his feet. 'You need a holiday.'

'No,' she said, turning to him so that she was silhouetted against the late afternoon light outside. 'I don't need a holiday. I need to work. I need to immerse myself in something— worthwhile. I can't bring my child into this.' She made a gesture with one hand.

'I can have it looked after here. Both of you.'

'No. I don't want to be looked after. I've been looked after. You've always been kind. It's not what I want. I don't think I ever did.'

'But we could rearrange things, rearrange the flat. There's room for a nursery. I shall be at home more, now that things are quietening down.'

She stepped into the room. 'Good God!' she said, great irritation in her voice and manner. 'You don't begin to get a glimmering of what I mean, do you? I don't want it. I don't want any of it. I don't want the comfort, I don't want protection, I don't want the shelter . . .'

'I see,' he said, lapsing into that resigned manner that infuriated her.

'No you don't! Why do you keep up this pretence? You don't see. You don't understand. You never have. You've never had the slightest insight into me. You've never made any attempt to understand.'

'I have tried,' he said.

'All right,' she said. 'You've tried. But I don't want you any more. I don't want to live with you. I don't want to see you again. I don't want any part of your philosophy. There's no newness in you. God laid down the pattern of British society on the sixth day, didn't he? That's what you genuinely believe, isn't it? And nothing can change it. No one must be allowed to hold any new ideas, to see any new shape. The function of government is preservation. But don't you understand? We've seen through it. It's hollow. You don't give a damn about people, do you? You really don't give a damn! Shape, form, pecking order—these are your beliefs. For all I care, you can toss the lot out of the window. Nobody will suffer—nobody but you. I wouldn't have a child of mine born into this mess for anything in this world.'

'I've really—truly—done the best I could.'

'That's the tragedy of it. If only you'd done your worst—your honest, sincere worst.'

'Where will you go?' He sat down again, slowly and a little painfully. He had given up. He had withdrawn from the contest.

'I don't know. To my sister's perhaps. But I don't know.'

She caught the boat train from Victoria that evening. Paine, out of a sense of duty and out of a wish to have nothing whatever to reproach himself with in future years, saw her off. She stood in the doorway of the carriage for a moment, looking down at him. She didn't say anything. They looked at one another like two strangers who had nothing whatever in common. When the carriage door was closed, she sat down in her seat and took up the evening paper. He watched the train pull steadily southwards out of the station. He put up his hand, but there was no answering wave. At last, when it had disappeared out of sight, he turned back towards the empty flat.

EPILOGUE

It remains for us in the North to sit out the present situation, for there is nothing we can do about it. Resistance groups are being organized, or so it is rumoured. But the Stars and Stripes flies over the central tower of York Minster, and Southern troops pillage the countryside.

One thing I should like to put straight. The Southern press has put out the story that I am being held under house arrest in Scarborough. This is untrue. I am being held in what remains of the old Debtors' Prison, under American guard. I cannot complain about the Americans. Their treatment of me is civil and courteous. They are, after all, only here to honour their treaty obligations with the Southern government. I sympathize with the difficult position in which they find themselves.

I have every hope that this manuscript can successfully be smuggled out of the country. My friend, Nicholas Leonard of the Cavalier Publishing in Dublin, is arranging for its publication in a neutral country.

ARTHUR WISE
Cell 4
Debtors' Prison
York